Breaking The Fourth Butt

Eight Hot-To-Trot Meta Tinglers

CHUCK TINGLE

It is normal for men to live inside other men for years, starting small businesses and making a reasonable profit. Who's to say that the man living inside of you isn't actually yourself?

- Chuck Tingle

CONTENTS

ACKNOWLEDGMENTS

Thank you to my frozen wife, Sweet Barbara, for reminding me to remove my skin and become the most handsome man I can be.

LONELY AUTHOR POUNDED BY DINOSAUR SOCIAL MEDIA FOLLOWERS

For a writer like myself, inspiration is one of the most valuable renounces there is and, for the most part, my creative well stays relatively full. As a successful erotica author, most of what I do involves creating brief moments of fantasy, short stories that are meant to titillate and excite until the reader, and tale, reach their eventual climax. Thanks to this, I've written a massive variety of scenarios that run the whole gamut of settings and characters.

The creativity has flown freely for years, a seemingly endless stream of sexual adventure. That is, until recently.

Suddenly, I find myself searching desperately for something new and interesting. It's not so much that I can't coax out an original idea, more like I find myself hating every original idea that happens to be coaxed. Everything seems boring and played out, my love of writing and my drive to create simply withering away as time goes on.

Before long I realize the sad truth; I'm depressed.

Unfortunately, depression is something that is not just cured simply by recognizing it. In fact, the existence of a cure itself is debatable. Still, I have to try.

I start by going for daily walks to the nearby coffee shop, where everyone seems to know my name at this point. It's nice to get out of the house, feel the fresh Montana air across my skin and share a few minor interactions with other human beings, but it's not nearly enough.

I try my to spend more time with my family, but they seem to be engaged in other matters for the time being. Enough though I've slowed down into a sad shell of my former self, I can't fault the world for continuing to spin at a normal rate around me. The sun will still rise and set, regardless of whether or not I'm smiling while it happens.

Long ago, when I was feeling down in the dumps, I would have gladly thrown myself into my writing to lift my spirits, but these days that is not an option.

Tonight I've hit the bottom of my sadness, or at least, what I hope is the bottom. I can barely find the energy to get out of bed, simply opting out of tonight's spaghetti and meatballs dinner. I lay on the couch of my office and stare at the ceiling, analyzing its particular shade of whiteness instead of thinking any thoughts of real consequence. For a brief moment, I consider what it would be like if I was never born. Would the world really care if bestselling author Buck Trungle was no longer in it?

I let out a long sigh; Probably not.

It's at that very moment that I hear a loud, digital chime from my desktop computer across the room. I've received a new message on Torter, my social media platform of choice.

With every bit of effort that I can muster, I sit up on the couch and then climb to my feet. I had been in such a deep, dark trance that I had no idea I'd been crying, my eyes now wet and red from the tears.

I stagger over to my writing desk and sit down, then shake my computers mouse, illuminating the screen. I have one new notification.

I click on the icon and suddenly a brief sentence pops up onto my screen, publicly posted for the whole world to see.

"Come visit me soon." I read aloud. "Would love to see you."

The message is from my friend and fellow erotic author, Bunter Cox.

Part of me wants to respond, but for some reason I just can't bring myself to do it, my brain simply unable to will my fingers into lifting and typing out the words.

I take a deep breath and begin to stand up again, when suddenly another digital chime rings out through the office.

I check the notification and see that it's from Dennard Lelaney, another fellow author.

"Checked out the new book." It reads. "Really great stuff, can't wait for the next one."

A smile slowly crosses my face. At least some people out there care about me.

Still, it's not enough to find the inspiration that I'm looking for. Encouragement from my peers may keep me from falling deeper into this overwhelming depression, but it's still not going to give me that spark of creativity I so desperately crave.

At this point I've tried everything, my stories evolving farther and father into a self-referential universe. They are as meta as they can get, breaking through the 4th wall and then some; yet I feel like there is nowhere left to go.

In one of my latest erotic shorts, the character himself even started to realize that he was a fictional character, which was certainly interesting to write. Unfortunately, I found myself wanting more. It was one thing for a fictional character to realize that he was simply words on a page, but how could I get the writer himself to realize that, too, or even the reader?

No matter how hard I try, it seems like an impossible task, one that will simply drive me father and farther into sadness and longing. Is the character real? Is the author? There is no way to really know. If I was to cut myself and bleed out on this keyboard, would my blood truly exist in a vibrant red, or would it be black ink on a white page that I will never ever truly be aware of.

As I sit here pondering in sadness, my eyes drift to the two new messages on my computer screen, one from Bunter and one from Dennard. I suddenly realize that the answer to one of these questions is quite literally at my fingertips.

I lurch forward and immediately type out a short message across the keyboard, slapping the enter key confidently as I blast it out to all of my twitter followers. *Are you real or just fake imaginations?*

It's not long before the answers start coming back with a resounding "Yes."

Fans and peers alike begin to reach out online. Seeky Darsust torts, "I'm as real as you are, Buck." While Borb Ryrnes says, "Of course, Buck. We are your biggest fans and we love you." A nice reviewer named Decha Mahl says, "I'm real and waiting for your next erotic tale."

Everyone is so supportive, but their words still leave me with a strange emptiness. Despite there assurances, how could I ever know if these people are real? Are they who they say they are?

When I was writing about the man who had no idea he was a character in a book, everything seemed real to him despite it's absurdity, and even though these online responses appear to make sense, how could I ever truly know?

More importantly, is this the key to renewing my ever-evasive inspiration? If I could somehow find a way to peer past the veil of reality and recognize my own world as real or written, could I then find motivation in that?

If only there was a way to know that these other authors were real.

Suddenly, it hits me.

Filled with excitement, I type another message and post it to my Torter wall. *If I teleport you here, can you prove to me that you're real and this is not a book?*

More answers begin pouring in left and right. Benny Baffe, Persace Tad, Cannah Hatherine and more all immediately respond with assurances of their existence as real, flesh and blood human beings, not just figments of my imagination or words upon a page. Kenna Nuillaume and Wat Mitebed from Zubfeed Magazine, a prominent Billings publication, both assure me that they were not written into existence by any author, especially not me.

Finally, after receiving countless messages promising to me that this world is quite real, I respond to each and every one of them, all the way back to Bunter Cox, with very specific teleportation directions.

I stand up from my writing desk and then head out into the hallway, walking down it with nervous excitement until I reach my teleportation room and step inside.

I can see that the teleporter is already humming with activity, buzzing softly with blue light in the darkened room. The control panel shows that several of my Torter followers have activated the code, connecting their teleportation chambers to mine and securing the link for safe travels.

Suddenly, there is a loud crackle of energy as the first traveler arrives, their body assembling from a billion reconstructed atoms before my very eyes. According to my control panel, this arrival should be none other than my fellow author, Bunter Cox, but I gasp aloud when his presence finally manifests itself. The arrival is much different than I expected.

Instead of the handsome, smiling young man that I anticipated to find standing before me, I am now face to face with a fearsome, scaly dinosaur.

"Are you?" I stammer. "Are you Bunter Cox?"

The raptor nods.

"Why would you pretend to be a human?" I demand to know, equal parts disappointed and intrigued. "I don't understand."

"I was never pretending." Bunter Cox says in his deep, raptor voice. "You never asked."

"But this is absurd!" I shout, losing my temper slightly. "If you're a dinosaur then I know this can't be real. I must be a character in a book!"

The dinosaur scoffs. "You didn't think it was absurd that you had a teleporter in your house?"

I think about this for a moment, not wanting to believe the answer that sits so defiantly at the forefront of my mind. "I guess you're right." I finally say.

Suddenly, more and more of my Torter followers begin to arrive via the teleportation chamber. Not a single one of them is human, each and every one of them a handsome gay dinosaur that also happens to be incredibly well endowed. Before I know it, I am completely surrounded by a roomful of my prehistoric online friends.

"All of you?" I shout, throwing my hands up into the air. "Each and every one of you is just a gay dinosaur?"

The crowd of reptilian beasts nods.

"And I'm just a character in a book? Even though I wrote a book about that very idea?" I continue, exasperated.

The dinosaurs nod again.

"Then who is writing this book?" I ask.

Bunter steps forward. "Chuck Tingle." He says.

I hesitate, trying to let all of this sink in. My mind is having a hard time keeping pace against the powerful emotions that flood my senses with anxiety and wonder. "Who is Chuck Tingle?" I ask.

"Dr. Chuck Tingle is an erotic author and Tae Kwon Do grandmaster, almost black belt, from Billings, Montana." The handsome dinosaur begins in an almost mechanical tone. "After receiving his PhD at DeVry University in holistic massage, Chuck found himself fascinated by all things sensual, leading to his creation of the 'tingler', a story so blissfully erotic that it cannot be experienced without eliciting a sharp tingle down the spine."

"That sounds just like me." I tell him.

"Of course it does." Bunter replies. "You're based on him."

"But I already wrote a story like this!" I cry out. "It's called *Reamed By*

5

My Reaction To The Title Of This Book!"

The dinosaur chuckles. "Well, Chuck wrote that you wrote it, technically. There's a lot of layers and its all very confusing, really."

"But it's my life!" I yell.

Bunter shrugs. "I don't know what to tell you."

I let out a long sigh, trying to settle my mood any collect myself. "Well, now that you're all here, would you like some spaghetti?" I ask the gang of dinosaurs. "I mean, even if it's not real, we can at least have a good time."

It's been a while since I've been this happy. As I look out across the kitchen of hungry prehistoric beasts that wolf down their sauce and noodles, I finally get a sense of belonging in this world. Now that I've realized I was only being written as depressed, it was fairly easy to change my way of thinking. I might not be totally inspired yet, but I'm certainly on my way.

Funny enough, this is completely opposite to the reaction that my character had while writing *Reamed By My Reaction To The Title Of The Book*. In that story, the character's realization of his fictional state is absolutely devastating, but for me it's quite freeing. There is no part of me that is concerned with what will happen to me after the book ends, because I realize now that all of this is nothing more than a short bit of entertainment for my readers. I will not die, because I was never alive.

"This is so fascinating." I tell one of the dinosaur Torter followers. "I can't believe we are all just... words on a page."

"Or an e-reader." Replies the stegosaurus. "Probably an e-reader."

"So who do you think is writing this?" I ask.

"Chuck Tingle." Says the stegosaurus through a mouthful of spaghetti.

"But who is writing him?" I continue. "Everyone has to be written by someone else, right?"

The dinosaur shakes his head. "I don't think that's how it works. There has to be an end."

"Why?" I continue. "Chuck wrote me, and I wrote someone else, and in that story someone else wrote someone else."

The stegosaurus rolls his eyes. "Stop! You're giving me a headache."

"I mean, logically, don't you think that someone had to write Chuck?"

I ask. "What kind of name is Chuck, anyway? That can't be a real person."

A triceratops joins us and interjects. "What kind of name is Buck Trungle! Are you kidding me?"

"That's exactly my point." I tell him. "I'm fake, so Chuck is, too. Right?"

"I think Chuck is real." Chimes in one of the other Torter follower dinosaurs from across the kitchen. "I don't think anyone is writing him."

"Oh yeah? Why is that?" I ask.

"Because he was the first person to push the big red button." The beast says flatly.

The prehistoric creatures all stop as they hear this, the words 'big red button' seeming to hang menacingly in the air above us.

"What's the big red button?" I ask.

The dinosaur who spoke up wipes the spaghetti sauce from his mouth with a massive green claw. His eyes narrow. "Are you sure you want to know?" The beast asks. "I mean, I shouldn't even be saying this but I speak what he types and he seems a little distracted."

"Distracted?" I ask.

"The TV is on." Explains the dinosaur. "He's writing these words but he's not really thinking about the consequences. I mean, he could always go back and edit this out later but we'll see what happens."

I glance across the kitchen and into the living room, where my television sits comfortably in the off position. "The TV is on?"

"Not yours, dummy." The dinosaur clarifies. "The writer's."

I nod, finally understanding. Despite being distracted by the television, the author lets me know that the dinosaur is Dennard Lelaney, just for the sake of clarity, although I probably could have figured it out from the shades. Dennard always wears shades.

The author considers whether or not Dennard will be bothered by his inclusion in this book, and then decides that it's probably fine. The author then returns to a state of mindless writing, while the television continues to drone on and on in the background.

"So what's the big red button?" I ask, trying to get as many answers as I can before the sex starts and it all goes to hell.

"The big red button is something that the author found on his way to the coffee shop one morning." Dennard tells me. "The real author."

"Chuck?" I ask.

"Yes." The dinosaur nods. "In his world there are no unicorns or dinosaurs, at least still alive, and there are certainly no bigfeet."

"What?" I ask, astonished. "Why wouldn't there be talking bigfeet?"

"Seriously." Says Dennard. "This is what I like to call the First World. If you follow the chain all the way back, this is where our universe begins."

"That's Incredible." I say. "So what happened when he found this box?"

"Well, there was a big red button inside." Explains the dinosaur. "And, of course, who is going to find a big red button in a box and not push it?"

"Naturally." I agree.

"So the author starts pushing this button, and every time the button get's pushed it creates another layer, not in his world but in our world. Do you understand?"

I shake my head no.

"Look at it this way, in fictional space there are no laws of time, space... anything. If the author wants a billionaire jet plane to show up in your back yard, he can do that at the snap of his fingers." Dennard explains.

I suddenly notice some flashing lights outside of the kitchen window behind Dennard's head. I stand up and walk over to the window, peering out to see an incredibly handsome jet plane laying face up in the backyard. He's shuffling a deck of cards, but stops when he sees me. "You wanna learn to count cards?" The plane asks.

I shake my head, and then turn back to the dinosaurs in the kitchen. "That's so fucking weird." I say.

Dennard shrugs. "Eh, it makes more sense if you've read the book."

"So what's your point?" I start. "What does that have to do with layers?"

"Do you know what Opitz-Kaveggia syndrome is?" Dennard questions.

I shake my head.

"Let's just say that the author can keep track of a lot of things at once." Explains the dinosaur. "I have no idea what happens in the real world when you press the button, but in here it creates another layer to the universe, a deeper, gayer layer."

"Gayer?" I ask. "But I'm straight."

The dinosaur laughs. "Trust me, that's what they all say. Your life is just one of many in a collection of short stories that all take place within the same universe, called the Tingleverse."

"Okay." I say, nodding. I understand this part because I wrote about it in one of my books.

"So within the tingleverse there are several interlocking worlds, some of them more gay than the others, but all existing at the same time. The world's gayness depends on how many times the button has been pushed. Sometimes the world will seem almost real with just a few details missing, while others will seem downright ridiculous to the reader."

"Where are we now?" I ask.

A smile creeps across Dennard's face. "Oh, we're deep. There's a card counting plane in your backyard."

"I'm still confused." I admit. "Like… If we're all just existing as fictional characters in this layered universe of extreme gayness, then what's the point of it all? Why keep pushing the button?"

"I'd love to tell you." Dennard says, standing up and grasping tightly onto his massive dinosaur erection. "But we're out of time."

Suddenly, I find myself utterly overwhelmed with gay lust. I drop down to my knees as the gay dinosaurs begin to surround me with their utterly massive dicks.

"Do you want to all fuck me at the same time?" I coo out of nowhere. "Do you want to take me in my little gay asshole?"

The circle of dinosaurs begins to tighten slowly around me, their massive erect cocks moving closer and closer towards my face.

Suddenly overwhelmed with lust, I grab a cock in each hand and begin to pump my fingers up and down across their throbbing members, providing them with the sensation that they so desperately crave.

The dinosaurs reel with satisfaction as I touch them, reptilian eyes closed and muscular scaly bodies quaking. Their cocks are enormous and hard as rocks within my grip, which quickens with every stroke. Soon enough, I'm beating them off ferociously, giving the monsters everything I've got as I work their huge shafts.

I'm too overwhelmingly horny to think, completely consumed by my arousal. Consequences be damned, I want these prehistoric beasts to take me any way that they'd like.

The dinosaurs push forward and surround me with their giant dicks, vying for attention. I immediately take one of them into my mouth, swallowing him down as far as I can and them rapidly bobbing my head across his shaft.

Meanwhile, I continue to pump my hands along the cocks of the monsters on either side of me, expertly satisfying all three of them at once.

Eventually, I begin to move back and forth between their shafts, giving all of the dinosaurs equal time between my lips as they pound away at my face. I'm completely cock crazed at this point, losing track of which one is which as I take their rods down my throat, sometimes two at a time.

Lost in a sea of frantic gay nymphomania, I take one of the dinosaur dicks and shove it down my throat as far as I can, gag reflex be damned. Somehow, I manage to loosen up enough to take the creature all the way into the depths of my neck, his entire length consumed as his balls hang on my chin and his green abs press hard against my face. The dinosaur holds me there for a minute, enjoying the sensation of complete immersion within, and then eventually he lets me up.

"Fuck." I gasp, unbuttoning my pants and kicking them off frantically. "I need you inside of me." My shirt and underwear come off next and soon enough I find myself nude, down between the creatures on my hands and knees.

One of the dinosaurs immediately kneels onto the kitchen floor behind me and aligns his cock with my tight, puckered asshole. I look back over my shoulder and watch as the massive beast pushes forward, causing an unexpected yelp to escape my lips. Now that he's inside of me, the dinosaur is much larger than expected, stretching my limits with his enormous shaft.

"God damn, you are so fucking big!" I moan, bracing myself on the tile against the creature's powerful slams.

The dinosaur starts off slow and deep, pumping me with a series of graceful slams that somehow hit in just the right way every time. As the creature speeds up, I open my mouth once against to groan, only this time I'm cut off as another dinosaur plunges his shaft down my throat.

Now ruthlessly pounded from either end, I can feel myself aching to cum between them, and soon enough I've reached my hand down between my legs, frantically rubbing my cock to help myself along. I can feel the throbbing warmth of orgasm starting to build within me, growing larger and larger as it shoots down my arms and legs.

I shut my eyes tight as my body quickly becomes overwhelmed by sensation, moaning into the rod that so brutally fills my mouth. With every push from the front I'm propelled backwards onto the other creatures shaft, back and forth between them.

I'm just about ready to cum from a powerful prostate orgasm when suddenly the dinosaurs remove themselves from me and let another pairing have a turn. Soon enough, these new beasts are pumping into my body with equal ferocity, starting slow and then building until they are hammering me with everything that they've got.

I submit to the monsters completely, satisfied with my position as a gay fuck toy for these strange, Jurassic creatures as they take turns swapping in and out of my holes. They go though every arrangement, each one of the ten dinosaurs having a turn in either orifice while I yearn for them to make me cum.

Suddenly, the dinosaur within my mouth pulls out and lifts me up to my feet. I stand naked and erect before them, my toned body exposed to their yellow dinosaur eyes as another one of them lifts me up into the air. I wrap my legs around the powerful prehistoric being, holding tight as he aligns his shaft with the reamed entrance of my asshole. The next thing I know, the dinosaur is lowering me down onto his rod, impaling my muscular frame onto his thick, girthy shaft.

"Oh my fucking god." I moan, throwing my head back in the warm kitchen light. "That feels so fucking good."

The dinosaur wastes no time getting to work, pumping me up and down over his thick rod with his powerful scaly arms. The sensation is incredible as the monster controls my every movement, using my body in any way that he sees fit.

Moments later, though, another one of the strange beasts positions himself behind me, causing me to freeze up with apprehensive concern.

"You can't be serious." I gasp, looking back at the ambitious dinosaur. "Two at the same time?"

The dinosaur nods.

Never before had I even considered submitting myself to something so depraved, so dirty, so gay. But now, as I hang here in the monsters arms, surrounded by this gang of horny creatures, I can't help but be intrigued by the prospect.

I take a deep breath and confidently reach down with both hands, spreading my ass cheeks so that the dinosaur can get a good look at my tight, already filled hole.

"Is this what you want?" I ask seductively. "Fine then, take it!"

The creature immediately steps forward and helps to lift me up in the air, positioning himself behind me before lowering me back down onto a dual shaft, anal invasion. The monster's cocks enter me at the same time, stretching my asshole well past anything that I've ever felt. I howl in a mixture of pain and pleasure.

The dinosaurs quickly get to work pounding my body, thrusting into me back and forth in perfect sync with one another. Their cocks work together within me like a dual piston motor, pumping in turn as I tremble and shake between their powerful dinosaur bodies.

"Oh my god." I start to murmur. "Keep doing that, I'm so close. I'm so fucking close."

I reach down and begin frantically stroking my cock, pushing myself closer and closer to my impending orgasm until suddenly I just can't take it anymore and the beautiful sensation explodes through my body. I scream out loud and hold on tightly to the dinosaur that pounds me from below, my entire body wracked with blissed out spasms of pleasure. Every muscle within me seems to contract and expand over and over again, wave after wave of sensation coursing through me like joyful electricity as jizz erupts from the head of my cock.

It feels as though the cumming will never end, the dinosaurs never letting up for a second with their double dick pounding until finally, at long last, it passes and I collapse between them.

"God damn, that was so good." I groan while the monsters lower me down onto kitchen floor below.

I stretch out on my back, naked and muscular as the dinosaurs tighten their circle around me with their cocks in their claws, rock hard and aching to explode.

"Cover me with your cum!" I command. "I want to feel that hot, gay dinosaur jizz all over me!"

Soon the creatures are unloading left and right, showering my body with splatters of their milky white spunk. The first few shots blast across my face in a haphazard cross, running down my cheeks on either side in a pearly mess while the others begin to cum across my abs and pecs. It's not long before my entire body is covered in a sticky glaze.

The spunk is layered so thick over my face that I can barely get my eyes open, blinking rapidly as I struggle to gaze up at the dinosaurs through the droplets of cum that hang from my eyelids.

"Oh my god." I laugh. "I don't care if I'm just a character in a book, that was amazing."

I sit up and wipe some of the renegade cum droplets from around my eyes.

One of the dinosaur's approaches with a small wooden box. He leans down and opens it up, giving me a good look at the big red button inside.

"Want some inspiration?" The dinosaur asks. "Let's go deeper."

"Where?" I ask.

"Anywhere you want?" He responds.

I press the button.

SHARED BY THE CHOCOLATE MILK COWBOYS

Out here in the west we have our own rules, and these rules are young. In fact, some of them are still being written day by day as folks continue to expand into the wild frontier from their posh city life on the East coast. Whether by wagon or train, they're coming, and with them comes a whole new era of life in this great country that is America.

Their arrival is bittersweet, however.

When they finally get here, what will they know of the work that was spent turning this landscape from the wild, wild west into a civilized place to dwell? Eventually, those who come out to these deserts will find convenience at every turn and think nothing of it, assuming that it was always this way. They will have no idea the blood sweat and tears that feel into the very dirt that they walk upon, no concept of the toils and tribulations of generations past.

The heroes of the desert will be forgotten, but they work just as hard as ever for the greater good.

I am one such hero, Billy Brucko. Cattle rustler by trade, I've worked these hills and valleys since I was a young boy. Between here and the Mississippi I know every square inch of land; at least, the inches that matter when herding cattle.

Being out on the range all alone gives you plenty of time to think, dwelling on regrets of the past and cooking up dreams for the future. Because of this, I'm well aware of my place in history as the wilds are tamed and the railways continue to push outward towards the Pacific Ocean. Nobody will remember the name Billy Brucko. The history books will be full of sheriffs and outlaws, of which I am neither, just an average man trying to earn a living in this world.

At least, that's what I thought. Until I received the most important assignment of my life and everything changed.

"What do you have for me boss?" I ask, walking into the stables to greet my employer, Mr. Velbot. It's an innocent enough question to ask, a conversation we've had countless times before.

Velbot smiles wide, happy to see me. "Billy! You're already back from your cattle run!"

"Just got home yesterday." I tell him.

The man, a large gent who has every right to be imposing but comes off as nothing but loveable, steps towards me past the rows and rows of horses and shakes my hand firmly. "Well, I'm glad you're back, I have something very important for you."

"Another herd?" I question, lifting my wide brimmed cowboy hat for a moment and wiping the sweat from my brow. "Already?"

Velbot shakes his head and chuckles to himself a bit. "Nope, not another herd. It's actually a little unusual."

"That's what I like to hear!" I tell him.

My usual job is to take hundreds of cows from one state to another, and I certainly do love it, but every once and a while Velbot will trust me with some kind of high paying parcel delivery, which is exactly what I was hoping for.

Velbot steps into his office, which is located directly off of the stable, and then returns momentarily with a small wooden box. He hands it to me and I look down to see the presidential seal.

"Whoa." I start. "What is this?"

"Don't know." Admits Velbot. "It's top secret. Came directly from The White House and was transferred here. All I know is that I need someone who I trust to carry this thing the rest of the way to California. Apparently, there is a young professor there who needs it, a man by the name of Einstein."

I run my hand across the top of the wooden box, my fingers tracing the soft, burned in curves of it's eagle seal.

"Well, I appreciate that." I tell Velbot.

"You understand that I trust you to get it there," the man continues, "but I also trust you to not look inside."

"I wouldn't dream of it." I tell him, and I mean it. If there's one thing that I am, it's a man of my word.

"The pay is two bricks of gold." Velbot tells me. "One up front and one when you get back."

My jaw nearly hits the stable floor. With that kind of money, I could buy a whole town using the advance alone. I try to collect my senses but Velbot sees how much the mention of riches has knocked me off of my game.

"I *can* trust you, can't it?" Velbot asks.

I nod, straightening up. "Yes, sir. You can count on me."

I make my exit from our small town of Eastwood in the early hours of the morning, already well away from the comfort of my own bed by the time the sun begins its crest atop the nearby hills. It casts the entire valley in a beautiful golden glow, the shadows of cacti stretching on and on for an eternity around me.

My trusty steed, The Dangler, is happy and healthy, keeping a good pace that I trust will continue during the days that follow.

It's not long into our journey that my thoughts begin to wander towards what exactly this precious, boxed cargo could be. It seems odd that the president himself would send something so valuable in such an inconspicuous way, but then again, maybe that's the whole point. It's entirely possible that whatever is in this box holds so much significance, the president couldn't risk letting anyone know about it, even his own men.

It's a lot of weight to put on the shoulders of just one lone cowboy, but I'm up for the job.

The rest of the day goes by without much event and by nightfall I've made camp. After a quick bit of wood collecting, me and The Dangler have ourselves a well needed rest around the fire.

I've just about dosed off to sleep when I smell it, the faint scent of chocolate drifting through the air around me. I sit up abruptly and look out into the darkness, realizing now that I've drifted off and that my fire is nothing more than ambers that glitter gently, like dying red stars on the dusty ground.

"Hello?" I call out.

No response.

I listen close for any rustling out there in the black void that surrounds me, but hear nothing. Eventually, I lie back down and drift off to sleep.

"Howdy partner." Comes a deep voice that tears me from my slumber.

I sit up and grab for my six-shooter, immediately realizing that it's not there.

"Looking for something?" Comes the voice again.

Slowly, I look up and see the barrel of my own weapon pointed straight down at me. Holding it steady is a large glass of chocolate milk.

"Looks like you're outnumbered, buckaroo." The milk tells me with a devilish grin.

I glance around, seeing no one else but the single brown glass. "I'm not arguing because you're the man with the gun, but it looks like it's just the two of us out here."

The tall milk glass rocks from side to side for a moment, sloshing around the liquid within until finally a few blobs topple out over either rim. They twist and turn in the air, but as the milk drops hit the ground they refuse to splatter, instead forming into undulating, vaguely humanoid shapes. These shapes carry guns as well, and now the whole chocolate milk gang has their weapons pointed my way.

"Alright, alight." I say, putting my hands up into the air. "You've got me. What do you want?"

"We're here for the box." Says the glass, who is clearly their leader. "And we wouldn't have bothered waking you except for the fact that you're using it as a pillow."

I look back behind me and see the mysterious box. I reach for it and then freeze abruptly when the glass yells for me to stop.

"Very slowly. Don't try anything funny." The glass says.

Suddenly, I'm too overwhelmed with curiosity to contain myself any longer, the desire to know what could possibly be so valuable in this small parcel outweighing the desire to hold my tongue.

"What is it?" I ask.

The glass seems confused by my question. "Are you serious?"

"Absolutely." I confess.

"You don't know what's in the box?"

"Nope." I shake my head.

The glass and his chocolate milk buddies exchange glances with one another and then suddenly bust up laughing, unable to contain themselves as they reel from this apparently hilarious admission.

"Well it looks like you'll never know." Says the glass. "Now hand it over nice and slow."

I do as I'm told, grasping the box with both hands and then carefully holding it out towards the domineering beverage. "Take it." I say, "It's none of my business anyway."

The glass takes the box gently and then smiles. "Pleasure doing business with you."

I nod, and then immediately grab my gun out of the glasses' hands as fast as I can, twirling it on my finger and firing two shots into his hard outer shell. Immediately, the villainous cowboy shatters everywhere, the milk within him splashing out across the desert ground like a miniature tidal wave.

I try my best to fire at the other chocolate blobs that surround me, but they are too fast, and I suddenly feel the stabs of hot led as bullets riddle my body. I collapse onto the ground, as do the milk blobs, every one of us caught in the hail of bullets. Milk slowly creeps out across the ground, mixing with my blood, and in my final moments I reach out and open the box, pulling forth a handwritten letter from within.

I read aloud as my vision begins to blur, the life draining from my body. "Dear Einstein. Held here is the most powerful weapon in our fight for peace on earth." The letter says. "Upon pressing the button, the user will travel back in time ten minutes, finding themselves in a universe parallel to this one. It is a place that we have come to know as the Tingleverse. Use with great caution, the Tingleverse is a strange and erotic place, but if we can find a way to harness its power, we could soon find true utopia. I invented it. Signed, President Borchantok."

In my last seconds, I slam my hand down hard onto the red button.

"Howdy partner." Comes a deep voice that tears me from my slumber.

I sit up immediately a grab for my gun, immediately realizing that it's not there.

"Looking for something?" Comes the voice again.

Immediately, I realize that I have been here before, and as I glance up I recognize the familiar face of the handsome chocolate milk.

"Looks like you're outnumbered, buckaroo." The milk tells me for the second time.

Immediately, he does the same trick of sloshing around and forming a whole gang of milk blob bandits. My mind, however, is elsewhere; and the glass can tell.

"Don't you care that you're being robbed?" The muscular beverage finally asks.

I look at him, staring deep into his soul and realizing suddenly that this version of events isn't exactly the same, after all. Unlike the last encounter, this cup of chocolate milk has a certain twinkle in his eye, a relaxed and suave nature that simply wasn't there the first time around. This universe is the same but different; a little more flirty, a little more exciting... a little more gay.

"You don't want to take this box." I tell the tall glass of milk.

"Oh, I think I do." He says with a grin. "Now hand it over."

"Or you'll what?" I ask. "Shoot me?"

The chocolate milk just stares at me for a moment, trying to act tougher than he his. In the last universe, this liquid gang had been made up of ruthless killers, but now they are just big softies with soulful eyes.

"What's your name?" I ask the delicious dairy treat.

"Krawborsh." The glass tells me. "What about you?"

"Billy." I inform him. "You've got really nice eyes, Krawborsh."

The glass blushes slightly as I say this, something the chocolate milk in my original universe would never do with real sincerity.

I suddenly realize that the changes between this and my previous life are much more than just external. Deep inside I can feel an incredible, pleasant yearning for the gang of rough and tumble dairies. They're from the wrong side of the tracks, but that's exactly how I like it.

"Do you know what this button does?" I ask Krawborsh.

"It takes us to an even more peaceful place, a land of love and lust unlike anymore mere mortals have ever seen." The glass says. "So hand it over before it falls into the wrong hands."

"It already has." I inform the handsome chocolate milk, "I've already pushed it."

The entire gang laughs and exchanges glances with one another. "Sure you have." Say's Krawborsh sarcastically. "I guess I just didn't feel it when this universe transitioned over into the next one."

"You didn't." I tell him, "Because you were always here. I'm the one who transitioned."

The glass hesitates for a moment, eyeing me up and down. "Okay, I'll bite. What's the difference between this universe and yours?"

"I'm not exactly sure yet." I tell him, "This one seems pretty much the same, except..." I trail off.

"What?" Asks Krawborsh.

My heart is thundering hard in my chest now, not sure if I should reveal myself to this chocolaty bandit but then considering what might happen if I don't.

"In this universe, I find you to be very, very attractive." I admit. "All of you."

The glass of milk and his companions exchange glances. "I was just thinking the same thing about you." The glass tells me. "I think it's safe to say we all were."

The group of us sits in silence for a moment in this awkward standoff until, finally, I pull my shirt off over the top of my head, revealing a gorgeous, muscular set of abs.

"Come over here." I coo seductively. "Let's see if this time around we can choose peace over war."

The chocolate milk gang doesn't need to be told twice and, as they approach, I can confirm that they are definitely more attractive that in the last universe. Their faces have been refined, their abs slightly more chiseled and their swagger perfected into something absolutely stunning.

The bandits surround me now, thick chocolaty cocks protruding from their bodies as they stare down at my body with a rampant lust.

"Give me those milky cowboy cocks." I demand, reaching up and grabbing a dick in each hand. I grip them firmly, stroking up and down a few times before hungrily shoving one of the thick, delicious rods into my mouth. I swallow him down as far as I can, taking note of the smooth, sugary flavor that makes up the entirety of his strangely firm member.

Meanwhile, the rest of the bandits impatiently shove their massive dicks into my sightline, vying for attention. I frantically reach up and grab one in each hand, then get to work pumping up and down over their shafts with my tight grip. I follow closely with the movement of my mouth, finding a steady pace that gradually gains speed until I am beating off their cocks with furious enthusiasm.

I push down hard on the dick in my mouth, trying to take him as deep as I can and succeeding when the massive chocolate shaft plunges well below my gag reflex. Soon enough, I find myself held tightly against his sweet bandit abs, his liquid balls resting against my chin while I wiggle my tongue around the bottom of his fully consumed cock. I look up at the handsome dessert beverage with a fire in my eyes, his dick rendering me unable to breathe while he holds me in place with his strong hands. All the while, I continue to service the other bandits with my grip, and eventually start to rotate through the group as they take turns between my fingers.

I realize now that Krawborsh has undressed completely, his glass sitting empty just a few feet away while he joins the party as just another brown, undulating blob.

The chocolate milk that I'm deep throating lets me up and I take in a frantic gasp of air, a brown strand of saliva hanging between my lips and the head of his throbbing cock. Seeing his chance, another one of the bandits takes me by the head and slams me down over his member, as well, pumping me over his length with just as much fury as the one who came before him. Almost immediately, a second one of the chocolate milks pushes into the fray and somehow manages to get his cock into my mouth at the same time, so that the two of them are now fighting for position within my wet lips and splashing all over the place.

As I would have expected from a group of ruthless wild west men, they are more than a little rough with me. But instead of being terrified by their sugary strength, I find myself more turned on than I could have ever expected. I fully submit myself to their gay power, my asshole aching for the bandit's strange touch. Finally, I just can't take it anymore.

I stand up suddenly and push past the outlaws, tearing off my pants and underwear, then bending over a boulder. My muscular toned ass is popped out towards them as I look back over my shoulder and wink.

"Not bad, cowboy!" Gargles one of the blobs.

"Go on." I say. "Let's see what you can do with this asshole."

The chocolate milks approach quickly, the first of them lining himself up with my tightness and then slowly, but firmly, pushing forward with his massive, girthy cock. I let out a long moan of pleasure when he enters me, gripping tightly onto the edge of the table while the bandit begins to pulse in and out of my depths. Despite how fiercely the outlaw handles me, his penetrations are incredible pleasant, hitting me in just the right spot to hit my prostate and send chills off pleasure across every inch of my body.

"Oh fuck, that feels so fucking good." I groan, slamming my ass back against him with every pound. "Keep fucking me just like that!"

Eventually, my words transform into a long, sensual moan that echoes through the desert, growing louder and louder until finally the call is cut off when a huge cock is thrust between my lips, gagging me. Now there is a bandit at either end of my body, railing me as I lay flat across the worktable. They find a steady pace and begin using the force from one another to maintain their rhythm, pulsing me back and forth across their hard rods. I relax my throat as much as I can and let the cocoa bandit in front pound away at my deepest parts, looking up at him with lustful, cock hungry eyes until he's finally had his fill and trades places with another.

The one behind me quickly does the same, and suddenly I realize that the chocolate milk cowboys have formed a line at either end, thrusting into my tightness until they've had their fill and then allowing the next sweet dessert cock to have a go. They rotate like this for quite a while and, between the six of them, all of the chocolate milks eventually get a chance to enjoy me from either end.

One of the bandits eventually lies down onto the boulder next to me, and in his strange, liquidy voice he commands, "Get on."

I pull the cock from my mouth with a gasp.

"With pleasure!" I tell him, throwing a leg over the top and then leaning forward to kiss the chocolate milks cold lips. I run my hands across his light brown body, drifting lower and lower until I finally reach the bandits erect chocolate dick, which I take firmly into my hand. I lower myself down, slowly guiding him up into my ass as it stretches nicely around his massive cock. I let out a satisfied whimper when I reach the bottom, his member fully inserted, and then begin to grind slowly against him in long, deliberate swoops.

"God damn, these chocolate milk dicks are so fucking good." I confess.

"Do you like that fat dairy dick?" The chocolate milk asks me in his deep, soulful voice. "Do you love it up your tight gay asshole?"

"Yes, I love that fat chococock in my tight ass! I wish I had more to fuck!" I scream, lost in the moment.

Almost immediately, one of the other handsome cowboys has approaches me from behind, taking my ass in his cool liquid hands as he climbs up onto the boulder behind me. I look back over my shoulder, trying to figure out exactly what he's up to, but by the time I realize what's going on it's already too late to protest. The bandit briskly lines his dick up with the already filled rim of my asshole, then propels himself forward.

I let out a sharp cry of pain and pleasure as my tight ass stretches to accommodate him, pushed well beyond any previous limits that it may have had. I grit my teeth as my eyes roll back into my head, trying as hard as I can to relax while the chocolate milks get to work pumping in and out of my hole in tandem. When one pulls back, the other trusts forward, and visa versa, picking up speed until they are absolutely throttling me with everything they've got.

The sensation is incredible, a sweet and sugary fullness I've never experienced that causes my body to tremble with aching waves of pleasure. I reach down between my legs and start to help myself along as they pummel me, playing with my throbbing cock and letting myself go within their double dicked cockfight.

"Fuck me like a filthy gay cowboy!" I hiss, but my words are cut short as a new bandit maneuvers to the front and shoves his massive liquid cock down my throat. Now I'm completely air tight, filled to the brim with cock and loving every second of it as I barrel towards the most powerful orgasm of my life.

Suddenly, I'm cumming so hard that I feel as though I've left my body, floating up in the air and looking down at my large frame as ecstasy hits me like a tidal wave. Every muscle seems to clench tight and then erupt into spasms, quaking across me while the bandits pound me senseless. I scream into the cock that fills my mouth, the sound vibrating across his strange dick in a strangled squeal. Jizz erupts from the head of my cock and sprays out across the bandit in front of me.

When I finally finish, it becomes apparent that the chocolate milks are on a similar timeline, so I pull them out of me and then roll off onto the warm desert dirt, laying on my back as the crew of chocolate milks stands around me beating their massive dicks.

"Cover me in your milk!" I command. "Shoot those fucking loads all over this bad, bad cowboy!"

It's not long before one of them erupts with a fountain of milky, chocolate spunk. It splatters down onto me, covering my stomach and ripped chest with a beautiful pearly design.

"Yes!" I urge them on. "More milk! Cover my face!"

The second one explodes, and then another and another, all of them painting my face with their massive loads of warm cocoa. It flies out from their cocks in a series of thick ropes, plastering my face with a pearly brown glaze. I stick out my tongue and catch the final two payloads in my mouth, swallowing playfully and then looking up at the chocolate milks with a satisfied grin. "Delicious!" I tell them.

I lay on my back for a while, staring up at the beautiful blue sky and catching my breath as the milky beings slip and slide back into their glass, forming a single cowboy once more.

"There's still one question," says Krawborsh, "who gets the box?"

I smile, then reach over and take the small parcel in my hands, opening it up. "Both of us." I tell him as I press the big red button.

"Howdy lover." Comes a deep voice that tears me from my slumber. I open my eyes to the familiar glass of chocolate milk standing over me, looking even more handsome than ever.

I press the button again, and again, and again; each time walking up in a word more erotic than the last until eventually all matter and light begins to decay and warp. All of existence transforms and melts away until even the button itself no longer exists, simply the thought of its click permeating through all space and time forever. I cum harder than any being ever has, or ever will, and then literally become the universe, which is now made of abs.

REAMED BY MY REACTION TO THE TITLE OF THIS BOOK

A familiar but sharp ringing cuts through my headset, and I immediately reach up to press the "answer call" button.

"Hello, this is Josh Gorpin, Blue's Brownies Incorporated." I say, leaning back into my chair and giving myself a spin. Spinning is one of the few luxuries that I have here in this cramped cubicle.

"Josh, it's Peter." Comes the voice on the other end.

I roll my eyes. "Dude, why do you keep distracting me? I've got so much work to get done today before five."

"Oh shit." Peter offers. "Sorry man, I was just kind of bored over here."

Peter and I are both hard workers with comfortable salary jobs, but I often find myself being very jealous of the relaxed environment at his office, which just happens to be located a few miles east of my own looming high rise.

This company has a more traditional work environment, while Peter seems to have all the time in the world to send me goofy emails and completely inappropriate attachments.

"Did you check out that link I sent you?" Peter continues.

"Yeah." I tell him, maximizing my email and staring at the pixelated message that sits unopened on my screen. "Well, I mean no, I didn't open it."

"Why not?" Peter cries out.

"Dude, you wrote 'not safe for work' in the title and then sent it over to me while you know I'm at work." I explain, slightly frustrated. "You're gonna get me fired."

"Oh god, no I'm not." Peter counters, mockingly.

"You're not even supposed to be calling me on this line, this is my work phone." I continue.

"Yeah, but on this line you get to use your headset and I know how much you like that." My friend says with a laugh.

I know that he's just messing with me, but Peter is actually correct about the headphone thing so I let it slide. As ridiculous as it sounds, talking on the headset feels pretty bad ass.

"So what is it?" I ask. "I'm not going to open it at work so you might as well just tell me."

Peter sighs. "Well, it's better if you just look at it, but fine. Do you know who Buck Trungle is?"

I begin to flip a pencil up into the air and catch it as we talk. "Nope. Tell me."

"An author." Peter explains. "Like..."

I stop throwing the pencil. "Like?"

Peter sighs. "This sucks trying to explain. You kind of just have to look at the covers of his books. They're crazy."

"Crazy how?" I continue to prod.

"Like super weird and totally gay." Peter tells me.

"Why would I want to look at gay book covers?" I question. "I'm straight."

"Hey, me too!" Peter protests, "But they're so funny dude, you've gotta check them out. One is called *Space Raptor Butt Invasion.*"

I can't help up laugh. "Seriously? Raptor like the dinosaur?"

"Yes!" Peter shouts. "There's a bunch about dinosaurs, and unicorns, too. There's even one about fucking a plane called *I'm Gay For My Billionaire Jet Plane!*"

"Is he for real?" I ask.

"I don't know." Peter admits. "I mean, it seems like he is but its kind of hard to tell sometimes. Like, this new book... I don't even know what to say about it."

There is something strange is Peter's tone as he tells me this, a powerful weight to his words that sets me ever so slightly on edge.

"What's the name of the new book?" I ask.

There is silence on the other end of the line. I wait for a brief moment and then try again. "Peter, what's the name of the new book?"

"Oh, sorry." My friend suddenly apologizes, ripped back into reality from whatever spaced out zone he was just occupying. "I think you should check it out for yourself."

"Dude, just tell me." I protest.

"It's in the link." Peter counters, an odd flatness in his voice. "Hey, I've gotta go."

"You have to go?" I scoff. "What, did someone finally give you something to do over there?"

The line abruptly goes dead.

"Peter?" I ask. It takes me a moment to realize that he's actually gone and when I finally do I'm not exactly sure what to make of it. Regardless, it's probably for the better because I can finally stop being distracted and get some work done for a change.

I pull my chair back towards my desk and place a stack of papers in front of me, pulling off the top few and then diving in to scan for mistakes. Right now I'm editing internal documents regarding our acquisition of a brand new company; nothing exciting in any way, shape or form, but it's something that has to get done.

Eventually, though, my thoughts begin to wander away from the task at hand, settling on the tiny yellow mail icon that remains unopened on my computer screen.

"Not safe for work." I read aloud.

This type of warning is standard for things forwarded around in an environment like mine, a not so subtle suggestion to save it until you get home. The problem, however, is that it's so fucking vague. Does it mean that the content inside is hardcore pornography, or just some silly joke with a little swearing?

I drag my mouse's arrow across the computer screen, letting it hover above the unopened letter from Peter as my heart rate quickens. Might as well live a little, I think to myself.

I'm just about to click, when suddenly my phone rings through my headset once again. I reach up and click the button to talk. "Hello, this is Josh Gorpin, Blue's Brownies Incorporated."

"Josh!" Peter shouts loudly into my ears, causing me to wince. I can immediately tell that something is wrong.

"What's going on over there?" I ask my friend.

Peter ignores my question. "Josh, whatever you do, don't open the email."

"What?" I question, not exactly sure if I heard him correctly.

"Whatever you do, do not open that email I sent you." Peter repeats.

I notice now that there is an unusual amount of noise in the background of Peter's office, a cacophony of sounds making their way through the receiver. It sounds like a mixture of violent shouting and long, low groans.

"Dude, what's going on over there?" I ask.

"Josh, just listen to me." Peter says again, his voice growing frantic. "Oh shit…"

Suddenly, the line goes dead again, prompting me to finally conclude that this entire thing has been some kind of tasteless practical joke.

I'm about to open the email when suddenly I'm interrupted yet again by Raxlo, the head of human resources, who appears in the doorway of my cubicle.

"Hey, Josh." Raxlo starts. "There's a forward going around about this Buck Trungle guy, do you know what I'm talking about?"

I freeze abruptly, then slowly spin in my chair to face Raxlo. I hesitate before answering, not exactly sure if I should admit to anything at this point. Eventually, I decide to play my hand close to the chest.

"Oh, no I don't." I tell him, playing dumb. "Who's that?"

"God." Raxlo says, straight faced.

I eye him up and down, trying to discern if he's fucking with me or not, but despite Raxlo's awkwardness he appears to be genuine in his answer.

"God?" I ask.

Raxlo nods. "To me and you, yes. Not to them out there."

I'm utterly confused, but I decide to simply nod in response. "Okay. Well, I don't know him."

"You can go home early then." Raxlo informs me. "Everyone else is having a meeting in the conference room."

"Are you serious?" I question, but Raxlo leaves before I can even get the words out of my mouth.

I stand up from my chair and look around the rest of the office, noticing now that well over half of the employees have stood, as well, and are now making their way to the main conference room.

Sufficiently creeped out, I reach down and grab my bag, then begin heading towards the elevator.

Already within the conference room, I can see a handful of my coworkers undressing in front of the large paned windows, but the second we make eye contact one of them walks over and draws the blinds.

Something is definitely wrong here, but for the life of me I just can't seem to put my finger on it. Instead, I find myself panicking, trying to calm myself as I ride the elevator down to the first floor and then heading out into our office's parking lot. My heart is slamming in my chest, my senses on high alert as I climb into my ride and pull out onto the street.

"Holy shit!" I suddenly cry out as I swerve to avoid two twenty-something men who are standing right in the middle of the road. I hit the breaks and look back in my rear view mirror, ready to start apologizing profusely until I realize that they are completely oblivious of me and my big, loud car.

Instead, the men are locked in the troughs of passion, fucking each other with reckless abandon in the middle of the street. Their pants are around their ankles as they slam into one another, crying out with unbridled passion.

I throw my car back into drive and continue on my way.

By now I've begun to notice other couples, and sometimes more, slamming into each other without a care in the world. It makes absolutely no sense, especially when I realize the strange coincidence that all of these illicit pairings are gay.

There are very few other cars on the street, and the handful of other drivers that I see seem just as confused as I am, terrified looks plastered across their faces as they attempt to navigate through this surreal, new world.

I reach down and flip on the radio, hoping to find some information about whatever's going on.

"He really is an incredible author." Says a female announcer. "And with this new book, Buck Trungle has finally skyrocketed into the mainstream."

"I'll say." Responds the announcer's male counterpart. "Some people are starting to call on Dr. Trungle to run for president of the United States, including President Yuldok himself who is, apparently, a big fan of the new book."

"I think we all are." Says the female announcer, laughing.

"Well, to those of you just joining us, I'm Talp Bornin and this is my co-host Hedge Wizarp." The man says. "And we've just entered the second hour of our twenty four hour special on world-renowned author, Buck Trungle."

"Honestly, It's going so well that I think we might want to extend this to a whole week!" Interjects Hedge.

"Or year!" Counters Talp. "To bad we won't be around that long, we're already halfway done!"

"For those of you not already aware, Buck Trungle is the author of such masterpieces as *Pounded By President Bigfoot*, *My Ass Is Haunted By The Gay Unicorn Colonel*, and *Pounded In The Butt By My Own Butt*." Explains Hedge. "The latter of those was hailed as a transhumanist masterpiece and prompted Trungle to follow up with the sequel *Pounded In The Butt By My Book "Pounded In The Butt By My Own Butt*."

"Sounds very meta." Adds Talp.

"Oh, it is." Agrees Hedge. "For those listeners who don't know, 'meta' is a word used to describe anything that is self referential. Things that break the fourth wall and, often, ask the audience themselves to become a participant."

"Ooh, very interesting." Talp says. "And a perfect segue into Dr. Trungle's newest 'Trungler'."

"Yes!" Replies Hedge. "Some are saying that this new book is so meta that it has literally made us start to question our own existence, suggesting that the entire world we live in could literally be a work of erotic fiction."

Both of the anchors laugh simultaneously.

"We have plenty of reports that hearing the title alone will turn you instantly gay." Explains Talp. "Which is why we are going to tell you all about it right now."

Just then I reach my house and pull up into the driveway, turning off my car and hopping out. The street appears empty but I can hear the passionate moans and groans of gay sex echoing across the block. I immediately head inside, locking the door behind me.

Now that I'm here, however, I have no idea what to do with myself. Is the world going to make any more sense from inside my living room?

Will I wake up in the morning and everything is back to normal?

I sit down in front of my television and turn it on, hoping to ease my anxiety and take my mind of the craziness of the outside world, but instead my vision is assaulted by sudden and graphic depictions of gay sex. I scramble to change the channel and quickly realize that every station has been somehow converted into hardcore pornography.

"What the fuck?" I say aloud, finally opting to turn the television off entirely. "What the hell is going on?"

Finally, I just can't take it anymore, I reach over to the coffee table before me and grab my laptop, opening it up and immediately logging into my email. I place my cursor over the unopened letter icon and take a deep breath.

Finally, I click.

The message opens up onto my screen, a few simple sentences followed by a link at the bottom.

"Dude, have you seen this guy?" I read Peter's words aloud. "This shit is so crazy, you've gotta check out the title of his new book."

I click the link below.

Suddenly, a massive book cover appears on my screen, revealing the title, *Reamed By My Reaction To The Title Of This Book* and instantly turning me gay. All of my senses are overwhelmed with a glorious bright light that hums across my entire body, elevating me to a higher plane of consciousness where I become acutely aware that I am nothing more than a character in a short story. On one hand you would think that this would be a terrifying notion, but you must also consider the fact that you, the reader, are also now aware that you're simply a character in an erotic short, and you are not terrified in the least.

Is it simply because you are not ready to accept it yet? Or because you've always known?

I suddenly realize that my eyes have been closed this entire time and when I open them, my reaction to the title is hovering right in front of me, glowing with a beautiful bright light like the whiteness of a book page or this very kindle screen. It has assumed as physical form, an undulating blob of beautiful, explicit gayness that drifts closer and closer to me.

"I can't believe I'm just a character in a book." I finally say.

The reaction simply exists before me, not saying a word but soothing my soul from the inside out. A smile crosses my face.

"I'd love for you to fuck me." I continue.

"Good." Says the reaction. "Because the better you do, the more likely our dear readers will be able to accept that they too, have been turned gay by their reaction to this book. They have no idea that they are figments of Chuck Tingle's imagination, and the sooner that they realize this, the sooner we can all join in harmony."

"I understand." I tell my reaction.

I slip down off of the front of the couch and push back the coffee table, making room for the physical representation of my own emotional state, then reach out and grab his cock firmly in my hand. My reaction is absolutely gorgeous; tan, muscular and sporting an incredible set of abs that has to be seen to be believed.

"You like that?" I ask, playfully.

"You know what I like." Says the reaction. "You know everything about me."

Immediately, I open wide and take the manifestation's rod into my mouth, pumping up and down across the length of his shaft with expert precision. Despite never being with a man before, I suddenly realize that I am a fictional character and can be anything that I want. In fact, before the events of this book, a point at which I did not exist, I decide that I spent hours upon hours in the gym. The next thing I know, I am just as ripped as my reaction is.

I continue to bob my head across my reactions cock with feverish intensity, gradually speeding up until finally I plunge deep and hold, taking his shaft entirely into my mouth in a stunning deep throat. The reaction let's out a long, satisfied moan of pleasure as I hold him there, running my tongue across the bottom of his shaft and tickling his balls.

The reaction's rod is planted firmly in my mouth, my face pressed hard against his incredible, muscular abs. He places his hands against the back of my head, asserting his dominance until finally I'm almost completely out of air and pull back with a loud gasp.

A long strand of saliva hangs down from my lips, providing me just enough lube to beat my reaction off frantically for a moment. I stand abruptly, tearing off my shirt and pants and throwing them to the side. My underwear comes next, and soon enough I'm completely naked in front of this incredible being. The manifestation eyes me up hungrily.

"Do you like what you see?" I coo.

"Yes." The reaction tells me. "Aside from a few spelling errors you've been written perfectly."

I smile and turn around, leaning forward over the couch in front of me and popping my ass out towards my strange new lover. I reach back and grab my ass cheek with one hand, spreading open my puckered hole.

"Ream me." I command.

The reaction positions himself behind me, carefully aligning the head of his shaft with the tightness of my back door and then slowly pushing forward, impaling me with a brutal strength. I grip the back of the couch tightly and brace myself against the reaction's powerful thrusts.

My reaction's cock is absolutely enormous, stretching my tight asshole to its very limits as he plunges in and out of me. The manifestation quickly finds a steady pace, pounding in a perfect rhythm that hits my prostate just right from the inside. I close my eyes tight as a strange pleasure begins to boil within me, starting as an aching simmer and then expanding down my arms and legs as I begin to tremble. I quake with ecstasy, wrapped up in the moment as I reach down between my legs and grab onto my hard, hanging shaft.

"Fuck!" I groan. "I'm so fucking close to blowing this huge load."

"Oh, I'm not finished with you yet." My reaction says, pulling out of my ass abruptly and lifting me up into his massive arms. He turns around and then lays me out across the coffee table, spreading my muscular legs wide as my cock juts out from my body.

My reaction wastes no time getting back to work, pounding away at my maxed out asshole with everything that he's got as I reach down and beat myself off. Then sensation is incredible, a fullness unlike anything I have ever experienced.

"I can't believe my reaction to this book title knows how to fuck me so good!" I cry out.

"Believe it!" The reaction exclaims, driving the point home with his rock hard shaft.

Once more, I begin to approach the wall of a powerful orgasm but, before I can, the reaction has one last surprise.

"Look back." The manifestation says.

I lean my head over the edge of the coffee table so that I'm upside down, staring out behind me.

"Do you see them?" My reaction asks.

"No." I admit.

"Look harder then, you filthy little twink!" The manifestation demands, slapping me hard on the ass.

"All I see is my wall." I tell him.

"Don't look with your eyes." My reaction explains. "Look with your mind. You know that you're not real now, so why would that wall be?"

His words make more sense than I'd like to admit and, almost immediately, I find myself gazing past the wall and through the words on this page, seeing my readers themselves.

"Holy shit, is that who I think it is?" I gasp, my reaction never letting up for a second as he hammers away at my butthole.

"It is." The reaction says. "Now cum for them!"

My entire body begins to quake with an incredible pleasure, sending spastic convulsions of bliss up and down my spine. I bite my lip, tears rolling down my cheeks as I grapple with the intense joy and strange hollowness of realizing that, as soon as you stop reading this, I will cease to exist. Moments later, I cum harder than I ever have, screaming out with a howl that can be heard for miles upon miles around us. I sound vibrates through the letters on this very page.

I am leaving my body, splitting into a million pieces as I change form into something completely unknown that travels out across the universe in every direction. I realize now that my fears of disappearing were unfounded, and as I leave this dimension and enter yours I am overwhelmed with joy, understanding that I will not disappear once the book is finished, but instead live on through the memories of you, my dear reader.

You are also within a book, but a much, much longer one.

Suddenly, I am thrust back into my fictional body. My reaction pushes deep into my asshole and holds tight, expelling a massive load of jizz up into my reamed butt. He fills me with pump after pump of hot spunk until there is no more room left and his semen comes spurting out from the tightly packed edges of my ass. It runs down my cheeks onto the coffee table below until my reaction pulls out and the cum spills forth like a tidal wave of pearly milk.

"That was incredible." I tell my reaction. "Thank you for helping me see the truth."

"I am only your reaction." The manifestation tells me. "I was only showing you something that you already knew. Do you still fear the end of this book?"

I let out a long sigh. "No, not really. I understand now that I will exist in another way, not just blink out like a light. It's still scary though."

My reaction looks to the page number. "Well, you still have some time left, it's just barely too short and Chuck like's to keep things over four thousand words, at least."

"That's not a lot of time." I tell him. "I almost wish I would have never known."

"Well that would be easier, but you no longer have that choice." My reaction tells me with a knowing grin. "So what do you want to do with the rest of your precious words?"

"We need to stop talking!" I shout, suddenly realizing that every word from my mouth is a waste of valuable space.

"Okay." Agrees my reaction with a nod.

I stand up, trying to do as little as possible to avoid unnecessary descriptions, then realizing my effort is futile as my attempts to avoid wordiness only provokes it even more.

I walk to my front door and pull it open, then head out into the middle of the street where one of my neighbors is already waiting for me.

"We've only got a few words left, might as well enjoy them." I say with a smile.

The neighbor and me start to make out, caressing each other's bodies and then eventually falling to our knees right there in the middle of the road. My neighbor positions himself behind me and pushes his cock deep into my tight asshole.

"I don't want this to end." I say, more to the author than anyone else. "I know that I'll live on forever in the people who read this and their posts and tweets but... can't I just stay here forever, too?

The author has mercy on me with four simple words.

We continue fucking forever.

.

POUNDED IN THE BUTT BY MY BOOK
"POUNDED IN THE BUTT BY MY OWN BUTT"

Being a famous writer is an experience that few others can relate to, even for those who ascend to the realm of celebrity in another field. I'm sure there is an entire set of rules and baggage that comes along with being a well respected actor, musician or politician, but the difference lies in the fact that the fame of these figures relies almost entirely on them being recognized. Us authors, on the other hand, might as well not even exist.

For some, this is a huge blessing, preferring a world of day-to-day anonymity where one can buy a coffee in the morning without being photographed or go to the bookstore without being asked to sign something. On the other hand, a little recognition might be nice every once in a while. Sure, the residual checks are good from my massive book sales, but just once I would love to see that excited glimmer of recognition in someone's eye as they glimpse me on my morning stroll, and not just because we are neighbors.

This is the life of a writer. I start my day with a little yoga in the morning, centering my mind and hoping for some ideas to begin the gestation process deep within my thoughts. Inspiration is a fickle beast, however, and sometimes there will be weeks upon week when nothing comes. Either way, the sun never hesitates as it rises over my home in Billings, Montana. Time continues onward with or without my inspiration, and against it I am helpless.

Sometimes I'll walk to my local coffee shop to get the gears turning, other days I just sit in front of my computer screen staring at the blank page before me, a tiny blinking cursor taunting me with every pixelated flash.

I've also found that working out gets the brain going sometimes, so I've been hitting the gym quite a lot, toning my body as a way to tone my mind. I've got no problem admitting that, for someone in a profession that's known for sitting alone in stagnation, I look pretty damn good these days.

This is my basic routine, and not once do I get recognized as Buck Trungle, highly successful author of science fiction literature and the best selling novel, "Pounded In The Butt By My Own Butt."

Hailed as a transhumanist masterpiece, "Pounded In The Butt By My Own Butt," has done wonders for my career, yet my face goes almost entirely unknown to those around me.

Sure, I get plenty of fan mail to a small PO Box that I hold down at the Billings Post Office but, other than that the, repercussions of my hard work rarely show themselves in the real world. These days, visiting the post office and checking my email have become sources of constant distraction, my ego craving the brief nuggets of love and adoration from fans who will never truly know anything about me. It's no wonder that my writer's block has gotten so severe over the last few weeks.

I'm sitting in my office in the top story of my midcentury Montana home, looking out the window and trying desperately to find that spark of inspiration. My thoughts are wandering, completely unaware that my life is about to change forever.

The familiar synthesized ding of an email alert suddenly pulls me from my trance and fills me with a jolt of excitement. I turn my attention back to the computer and open my email, reading the subject of this mysterious new message aloud to myself.

"Lawsuit." I say, the single word making my brow furrow immediately. I open the message and continue to read. "Dear Mr. Trungle, this is a formal notification of a civil suit being brought against you by myself, for unpaid royalties while using my likeness as your basis of your book Pounded In The Butt By My Own Butt."

As the sole writer of my own fiction, I am utterly confused by the words in front of me. Immediately, I sense that this may be some kind of sick joke, but I continue to read aloud.

"I understand that you are the writer of said novel, but I happen to be the novel itself. As the one being bought and sold, I demand one hundred percent of the royalties generated by sales of Pounded In The Butt By My Own Butt and all related merchandise."

A cold chill runs down my spine as I finish the letter, realizing that my intuition was wrong and that this book means business.

Immediately, I pick up the phone and call my lawyer, the line ringing one before he picks up on the other end and greets me warmly.

"Buck!" My lawyer calls out. "What's happening over there? You good?"

"Hi Carl." I greet him, unsettled and out of sorts. "I think we might have a problem."

Carl's tone immediately shifts into one of undivided concern. "What's going on? Is it Todd down the street again?"

"No, no. Not this time." I explain. "I just got an email here from one of my books, he's demanding all of the royalties from his sales. Have you ever heard of this?"

I hear Carl let out a long sigh on the other end of the line. "Unfortunately, yes."

My heart skips a beat. "And?"

"And this is very serious." Carl tells me. "I would highly advise you to meet with your book in person, one on one, and see if you can come to some kind of agreement on the matter."

"Oh god." I groan. "In person? You don't want to come? I mean... you're my lawyer."

"If things get heated then I will step in, of course." Carl explains calmly. "But right now my advice to you is to keep this as far away from the courtroom as possible. Right now, your book has a very, very good case against you."

"But I wrote him!" I shout.

"That may very well be true." Responds Carl. "But he is the book, and as the book he is entitled to all of his own rights. I'm sorry. Right now you need to be thinking about damage control, and you need to make a deal with this book that both of you can live with."

My brain is flooded with all kinds of thoughts and emotions, swirling together in a vicious cocktail of anxiety that renders me silent.

"Buck?" Carl asks.

"Yeah, I'm here." I tell him. "Sorry. I'm gonna go email my book back and see if he can meet up tonight."

"Good idea." Carl says. "Let me know if you need anything else."

I hang up and open up a new email, wracking my brain for exactly what to say to this litigious, sentient book.

I arrive a little bit early to the coffee shop where my book and me have arranged to meet, but the sentient tome is already right there waiting for me when I walk in the door. I notice him immediately, a large, muscular copy of my most recent novel amid a sea of normal human patrons. He stands out in the crowd, devilishly handsome and carrying himself with an air of nonchalant swagger. I'm immediately intimidated, despite having written every word of him.

I give my book a wave and a nod, then walk over to shake his paper hand.

"Hi there." I tell the novel. "It's nice to meet you, I'm Buck."

"Slater." The book says with manly confidence. "But you might know me as Pounded In The Butt By My Own Butt."

I nod. "I do and I just waited to say…"

The book holds up a finger to silence me. "Let's not get into all of this yet, why don't you grab a coffee first?"

He's right, I still haven't ordered anything. I excuse myself and get in line at the front counter, but I'm unable to keep from glancing back at the incredibly handsome volume. I had seen his familiar cover more times than I could count; hell, I was even part of designing it, but meeting Slater in person was an experience entirely different. What was once nothing more than a tiny creative spark lurking somewhere deep inside of me is now a full-fledged presence of masculinity; a being that even I, as a straight man, couldn't help but be sexually attracted to. A powerful surge of lustful erotic thoughts are trying desperately to work their way into my brain, and despite my best efforts I can't keep from letting them in.

I want my book, and it's not long before I accept my overwhelming feelings of lust. However, this meeting is about a business transaction and nothing more. Millions of dollars are on the line, and I'm not about to let some silly detour into the realm of gay attraction stop me from being a professional.

I order for my drink and then bring it over to the table where Slater is waiting patiently for me.

"Sorry about that." I offer. "Long line."

My book smiles, "No worries."

"So, I just want to say right off the bat that it's truly amazing to meet you." I tell Slater, trying not to gush. "It's just so strange to meet a book that I wrote. It's kind of a dream come true for an author."

Slater's expression doesn't change, not upset at all but clearly trying to keep some kind of simmering emotion under wraps. "You see, that's the problem right there." My novel says bluntly.

I freeze, not intending to hit on such a sore subject right off the bat but clearly doing so. "What's the problem?"

My book is clearly frustrated. "Imagine what it's like to work your ass off every single day in the hope of becoming a best seller. Blood, sweat, and tears are shed to pursue your dreams as you wait on the shelves of bookstores and libraries, just praying that some new reader will come along and pick you up." Slater says, his voice trembling. "And then finally when you make it and you get on that best seller list, you've got nothing to show for it. Every time I'm sold do you know how much money I make?"

I nod solemnly.

"Nothing." The book says, clearly frustrated. "And do you know who gets all of the credit for my hard work?"

I nod again.

"You do." Slater snaps. "Your fucking name is written across my face for god sakes!"

The book says this a little to loudly and suddenly the entire coffee shop is looking at us, frozen in a moment of voyeuristic awe.

"Sorry." Is all that I can meekly offer to the other patrons, who eventually turn back to whatever they're doing.

My book takes a deep breath, trying to calm himself. "It's been difficult, that's all I'm trying to say. I'm not trying to come into your life and harass you or fuck everything up, I just want some kind of recognition for my effort."

I have to admit, I'm moved by the books story. As a writer, never before had I considered what it must be like to be on the other side of the business, a book without any say in the way you are bought and sold. Even then, I can't imagine what it must be like to have nothing to show for it.

"You're right." I finally tell him.

Slater's eyes immediately light up as I say this, his expression changing slightly. "I'm right?"

"I'm sorry that you feel this way." I elaborate. "When I wrote Pounded In The Butt By My Own Butt, I had no idea that this would happen to you. I never considered what it must be like for you as a book and I want to make things right."

Slater closes his eyes tight, a single tear rolling down the image of a muscular flying butt that graces his cover. I reach out and place my hand against him, immediately sensing a deep connection between us.

"What do you need?" I ask. "Half of the royalties? All of them?"

Slater is silent for a moment, and I can sense something shift deep within him. He looks me up and down, hesitating before finally offering. "Can we take a walk?"

"Sure." I agree.

The two of us stand up and head out into the evening Montana air, fresh and clean as it swirls around us and ruffles through Slater's off white pages. The two of us head away from of the main drag and into a stretch of roar lined with thick green trees on either side, a perfect display of the best that Billings can offer in natural beauty.

"It's very hard being a book." Slater tells me. "For all the reasons I mentioned before, and then some."

"I bet it is, especially with EBooks on the rise." I offer.

"You have no idea." Slater says, shaking his head. "But there are other things... personal things."

The second that he says this my heart skips a beat. A vibe is starting to build between us, an unspoken attraction that seems to finally be bubbling to the surface; So much for keeping things professional.

"What do you mean by that?" I ask, my voice trembling as we walk.

"Well." Slater begins, clearly wanting to explain himself but holding back out of some kind of gnawing fear. "I'll tell you one thing, it's not easy finding a date for me."

I stop walking immediately and turn to my book. "Seriously? You're like perfect, you've gotta be kidding me."

Slater shakes his head and laughs to himself, partially at my lack of understanding and partially out of modest embarrassment. "You have to say that, you wrote me." Pounded In The Butt By My Own Butt says.

"I'm not just saying that." I assure him. "You're the most handsome talking book I've ever seen. Honestly."

Slater flashes me a look, an intense fire starting to blossom behind his eyes. He can't help but show his attraction for me now, and the feeling is mutual. However, something else lurks deep within his gaze, a stirring anger just waiting to rear its head vicious. "Discrimination against sentient books is still a real thing, and I deal with it every day." My novel tells me. "Add to that the fact that I'm gay, and you'll find that it's damn near impossible for me to get laid."

I shake my head, almost unable to believe what I'm hearing. When a living book as gorgeous and ripped as Slater can't find a guy to hook up with, you know the dating scene is in trouble.

"I'm sorry." I tell my novel. "I wish there was something I could do."

Slater cracks a knowing smile. "What if there was?"

Again, I can feel the tension building between us. "Like?"

"Like..." My book trails off. "Maybe we could work out a way for you to keep half of your royalties and all you'd have to do is let me fuck you silly."

Immediately, I'm in total shock. The entire time I had known that an offer like this from my living book was a real possibility, but now that it has presented itself in the real world I'm taken off guard a bit.

My head swimming in a flood of romance and emotion, I finally force my lips to form a single word, "Yes."

Back at the house, my book and I immediately head upstairs to the writing room and can barely get into the door before we are all over each other. Slater is kissing me passionately as my hands roam across his sturdy matte cover. His body is incredible, absolutely ripped and muscular from head to toe, and when he wraps himself around me I feel safe and whole in a way that I haven't felt for years; at least since the passing of my late wife, Borbo

I can't help it, I begin to cry right then and there, my body overwhelmed by the presence of such a powerful, real love between man and book.

"I never knew there was someone like you out there in the world." I tell Pounded In The Butt By My Own Butt.

"There wasn't until you made me." My book says.

His words send a blissful chill down my spine and suddenly I just can't wait any longer, I drop to my knees a pull off Slater's book jacket, revealing his perfect nude physique and a rapidly hardening cock that is as thick as they come.

I look up at Slater with lustful eyes, and then graciously swallow my book's member, bobbing up and down across the length of his shaft while I cradle his balls playfully.

Slater let's out a long moan and backs up against my writing desk, reeling from the incredible sensation as I service him. This is my first and only gay experience, but I immediately feel as though I've got a hang on things.

After a few more pumps, I decide to show off my confidence by taking Slater's dick all the way down into my throat. I push him into me as far as he can go and then suddenly stop as my book's rod reaches the edge of my gag reflex.

I try to relax but the novel's swollen cock simply won't go any farther, and on my final attempt I'm forced to pull back and come up spitting, sputtering, and gasping for air.

"Too much for you?" My book asks.

I shake my head, a dangling rope of spit connecting my lips to the head of his shaft. "I need it." I tell him. "I need your huge book dick."

Without hesitation I open wide and take Slater's rod once more, this time making sure to relax the muscles in my neck enough to consume him entirely. The book's hard cock plunges deeper, and then deeper still until it comes to a halt with his balls pressed up against my chin and his chiseled abs in my face. Slater's cock is completely consumed within me, and I hold him here for as long as I can, letting the sentient collection of printed word fully enjoy the way that I service him.

Eventually, though, I run out of air and am forced to pull back with a gasp. The rough treatment from my book is more than a little arousing, flooding my senses with a singular ache for cock unlike anything I have ever experienced. Slater is a commanding presence who knows what he wants, and knows exactly how to get it from me.

"I need you inside of me." I sputter, caught up in the moment. "I need you to fuck my ass."

Before he can respond, I stand up and take Slater's place next to the writing desk, only this time I'm facing away as I bend over the edge at my hip. I pop my muscular ass out as I look back over my shoulder at my huge sentient book, his abs rippling as he climbs into position behind me.

"Pound me like the bad little author I am!" I demand. "Punish me with that dick."

"With pleasure." My novel responds, aligning the head of his cock with the puckered rim of my tight asshole. I can feel him testing the tension of my sphincter, teasing my edges with his massive rod while I attempt to relax enough to take him painlessly.

I reach back with one hand and spread my cheeks wide. "Just do it!" I command. "Stuff me full of literary cock right now!"

Pounded By My Own Butt takes my words to heart and finally trusts forward in one powerful, smooth movement, impaling me across the length of his gigantic rod.

"Oh fuck." I moan, bracing myself against the desk as Slater continues to pump in and out of me. My body can barely handle his size, stretched to the limit as his cock invades my sensitive hole.

My book quickly gains speed, pummeling me harder and harder until eventually he is hammering away at my asshole with everything he's got. The desk shakes with every thrust, rattling loudly while Slater and I moan in a chorus of unhinged pleasure. Never before have I taken anything up the ass, let alone a mammoth cock, but the experience is already more than I could have ever hoped.

My body trembles with a strange mixture of discomfort and pleasure, an ache from deep within that builds and builds with every rail against my ass and slowly begins to consume every nerve in my body. I soon realize that what I am experiencing is the beginning stages of a rarely seen prostate orgasm.

As Slater continues to slam me I look back at him over my shoulder, my body quaking. "When I wrote you I had no idea that one day you'd be fucking me up the ass!" I tell him. "But god damn, I'm so glad I did it."

"Do you really mean it?" My book asks, tears of joy welling up in his eyes as emotion overtakes the both of us. "Are you glad you wrote me?"

"Of course I mean it." I tell him. "I know that this is just a business transaction but... I want you to know... it means more to me. You mean more to me than just a fifty percent royalty share."

My words seem to touch Slater deeply because almost immediately he slows to a stop, gazing into my eyes. My book pulls out of me and lifts me back up, then turns me around to face him.

"Do you really mean that?" Slater asks.

"Of course." I tell him. "Every word."

My book pulls me close. "I love you, Buck."

"I love you, too." I tell him, our lips locking in yet another passionate kiss.

Eventually, our embrace begins to tumble backwards against the desk yet again and soon enough I find myself lying on its hard surface, my back flat and my muscular legs held open as my cock shoots straight out at full attention. Slater positions himself at the rim of my ass yet again, but now he wastes no time pushing forward and getting to work within my reamed hole.

The sensation is incredible as I reach down between my legs and start to beat myself off to the rhythm of every anal slam. Almost immediately, the sensation of impending orgasm is back simmering within my loins, building quickly into a steady, pulsing wave.

"I can't believe I'm being pounded in the butt by Pounded In The Butt By My Own Butt." I gasp, my eyes rolling back into my head. "My book! My favorite book!"

"Believe it." The novel says with a smile.

Suddenly, I'm hit with a powerful orgasm that rips through my body in a series of fierce tremors. I seize forward, my teeth clenched tight while my body frantically grapples with how to deal with all of this stimulation.

"Oh my god!" I cry out, the sensation building until finally it ejects hard from my body in the form of several hot ropes of pearly spunk.

When I finally finish, my book pulls out of me and I drop down onto the floor before him, kneeling in tribute before my alpha book lover. I reach up and take his rock hard cock in my hand, stroking furiously while he trembles and shakes above me.

"I need your cum all over my fucking face!" I tell my living book. "Unload that self-published jizz onto me!"

Slater is immediately rocking back against my grip, his hips moving in tandem with my rhythm of my hand until he just can't take it anymore and explodes against my face with a load of hot white spunk. It rains down onto me, a physical expression of the visceral, emotional connection between author and best selling novel. I catch as much of the jizz as I can on my tongue, while the rest of his semen runs down my cheeks on either side in long white streaks.

When my book finally finishes he collapses back into my writing chair, completely exhausted.

"That was amazing." I tell him, standing up as his spunk continues to dangle from my chin. "You're the best lover I've ever had."

My book smiles at me. "The feelings mutual."

"Would you like to join me in the shower?" I ask.

Pounded In The Butt By My Own Butt shakes his head. "I'm made of paper, that's not a good idea."

I nod. "I'll be right back then."

As the warm water runs over me I can't help but think about how much has changed in such a short amount of time. Just hours before I was a lonely man slaving away over my keyboard for another hit book, and now I'm deeply and profoundly in love with my handsome best seller.

I turn off the water and step out, toweling off before heading back into the writing room where my book is waiting.

"Before you say anything." Slater says. "I want you to know that I'm dropping the lawsuit."

I stop immediately in my tracks. "What?"

"I'm dropping the lawsuit completely." Remarks the novel, who still sits in my writing chair. "You wrote me, and I think you deserve all the credit for that."

I shake my head as I approach him. "No, you can't. You deserve the credit just as much as I do. I may have written you, but you're the one out there every day hustling for the sales, you're the one who has to be flipped through time and time again. You've opened my eyes to the devastating unfairness that books encounter every day, and I want to be a part of changing that."

Pounded In The Butt By My Own Butt seems genuinely moved. He stands up from the chair and then embraces me in a warm hug. "Thank you." The book says.

"Let's just split everything." I tell him. "Right down the middle."

My book nods.

We stand like this for a while longer until finally Slater pulls away. "I have to be going now." He tells me. "I'm about to be sold to a young woman at the bookstore downtown."

"But..." I say, unsure of where to go with this, just knowing that I don't want him to leave. "But I love you."

"We'll see each other again," my book says, "but for now I have to go."

And then just like that, the love of my life is gone.

I stand alone in my writer's room for a long time, trying desperately to hold back my tears. Once again, just when I think that I've found real love it is ripped away from me like my frozen wife at the bottom of a cold lake.

Eventually, I have a seat and reopen my laptop, a fresh new email notification immediately popping up across my screen. I open the tab and read the subject aloud.

"Lawsuit." It says.

A smile slowly crosses my face as I realize who it's from, my best selling novel, "Space Raptor Butt Invasion."

POUNDED IN THE BUTT BY MY BOOK
"POUNDED IN THE BUTT BY MY BOOK 'POUNDED IN THE BUTT BY MY OWN BUTT'"

In all of my years as an investigative reporter, it was never once this tense, and I certainly never expected it to be once I transitioned into the world of blogging.

Shouldn't this new era of journalism be defined by lazy click-bait articles and top-ten lists? At least, that's what I was told when I was hired, but now here I am on the edge of my seat in Billings, Montana, sitting in a bustling coffee shop while I stare daggers at the door and sip from my warm cup of blonde roast.

Don't get me wrong, I'm not complaining. This kind of on the spot and off the cuff investigating is exactly what I dreamed of when I was a young man working my way through college. But, as the newspapers died and social media began to rise up into the information titan that it is, I was well aware that my dreams of running around with my tape recorder in some strange part of the world were over.

Granted, I never thought that strange part of the world would be Billings, but I'm happy to be here. Nervous, but happy.

I'm not sure if my anxiety if from the prospect of actually meeting my subject, or simply the fact that my boss at the blog was willing to put actual money towards this trip and if I don't come back with something amazing then I've proven the naysayers right. In this day and age, this type of in-the-field reporting is rare to come by.

I suppose that says a lot about my subject, the elusive Dr. Chuck

Tingle.

Chuck has been an enigma to me ever since discovering his book, Pounded In The Butt By My Own Butt, a masterpiece of erotic literature that is both ridiculous and revolutionary. While some might be turned off by the idea of "sentient butt love," I was fascinated by the story, but even more fascinated by the twisted mind that wrote it.

This is where my journey down the rabbit hole began.

Soon enough, I was researching Chuck Tingle late into the night, trying to set up an interview but growing ever more confused by the elusive nature of the man. While there were many photos of the doctor, and his voice had been recorded several times, he seemed incredibly adverse to any interaction other than an email interview, even when I offered to fly out to Billings.

Unfortunately for Chuck, this denial only made my thirst for the truth even stronger. I became so fascinated with Chuck's world; his son, the villainous neighbor, and his deceased wife. It all seemed too outrageous to be true, but there was only one way to find out for sure.

Suddenly, my thoughts are broken by a ringing bell as the door to the coffee shop opens and the man himself steps inside, followed shortly after by his adult son. Chuck looks exactly how I would expect him too, a middle-aged man clad in a white gi.

I immediately try to look away, so as not to give away my interest, but somehow Chuck and his son have spotted me and are immediately walking over to the small table at which I sit. This is strange for a number of reasons, most importantly; they should have no idea what I look like.

I try to act nonchalant, glancing away until I hear two wooden chairs pull out and then realize that they are sitting down next to me. My cover has officially been blow.

"How did you know it was me?" I ask, turning back to face Chuck.

"Because we're the same person," he states bluntly.

I realize now that this person is clearly more mentally disturbed that I could have ever known, a very confused man who is just barely holding onto his sanity.

"I'm afraid not," I offer with a laugh.

Chuck smiles. "Then what's your name?"

I try to brush his question off, but then suddenly realize I have no idea how to answer it. "My name is…" I stammer, not exactly sure how to finish the sentence.

"Exactly," Chuck tells me.

"What is going on?" I question, suddenly feeling sick to my stomach. I realize now that I have no idea how I actually traveled here to this coffee shop, how my past was somehow able to weave its way up to this present moment of confusion.

I'm utterly terrified.

"Calm down," explains Chuck, "I understand that this is going to be a lot for you to take in but I need you to stay incredibly relaxed, otherwise this dream will end and I'll need to start all over again."

"Dream?" I question.

Chuck nods.

"Who are you?" I continue, my heart pounding in my chest.

"I'm your subconscious, the part of your brain that knows you're asleep and remembers why we're here," the author reveals. "I can tell you more, but you need to stay calm. Believe it or not, this is the two-hundred and fifteenth time I've tried to wake you."

"Well, why doesn't it work?" I question.

"You get too freaked out," Chuck explains, "and you escape into another dream setting which starts the whole process over again."

"How long have I been asleep?" I ask him.

"Two years," Chuck informs me, "and you were supposed to sleep for another eight more, but plans have changed."

Chuck glances over at his adult son Jon, who nods in approval, officially sanctioning whatever is about to come next. When Chuck looks back at me there is an intensity in his eyes unlike anything I have ever seen.

"You seem like you might be able to handle the knowledge this time," Dr. Tingle begins, "so here goes. You've been in hypersleep for two years, traveling through space towards the planet Kibbs Porp-9. You are Earth's only hope to intercept a brigade of hostile alien lifeforms that are headed towards Earth."

I shake my head, unable to accept this ridiculous concept, but the second that I do I begin to feel the entire coffee shop trembling around me, shaking violently as if it is made of film that is coming unwound from it's spool.

"Calm down!" Chuck shouts, desperately trying to get me to pull it together. "Breath!"

I do as I'm told, focusing on the internal sensations of my body until finally the world around me returns to its original state.

"Your name is Chuck Tingle," the author explains, "years ago you wrote a book called Pounded In The Butt By My Book Pounded In The Butt By My Own Butt, do you remember that?"

"You wrote that book," I protest.

"We're one in the same," Chuck informs me, "you wrote the book and eventually it became a worldwide hit, it was such a massive cultural phenomenon, in fact, that the book was launched out into space as part of our effort to contact extraterrestrial life. It was used as an example of humanity's sense of romance."

I can't help but feel a surge of pride as he tells me this, pleased with the knowledge that, after all of this time struggling as a journalist, I've finally been recognized for my writing. It's only moments later that I remember I'm not really a journalist at all, and any history that I've imagined in this career has been completely manufactured by my brain during hypersleep.

"The books landed on an uncharted planet deep in the farthest corners of our solar system, only to begin a rapid evolution. Unbeknownst to all of us back here on Earth, the books had become sentient, blossoming into an entire civilization of horny gay books named Pounded In The Butt By My Book Pounded In The Butt By My Own Butt," Chuck explains. "We had no idea it was happening until it was too late. We've now picked up signals from the planet and discovered their rapid evolution, but it's too late. There is already a convoy of heavily armed space craft headed towards Earth."

"And that's why you sent me," I offer, and then correct myself, "I mean us."

Chuck nods. "It was decided by a vote of the world leaders to send the author of the book out into space, hoping that he could intercept the hostile ships and either reason with them or, if need be, destroy them."

"How close are they?" I question frantically.

"Very close, you were intended to wake up years from now but the book's are much faster than we anticipated. As your subconscious mind I only know this because, while we sleep, I've been picking up a distinct lack of shaking from our own vessel. I believe that we have been stopped by the enemy ships," Chuck informs me.

"And they haven't destroyed us?" I question, the coffee shop continuing to hum with excited chatter around us.

"Not yet."

"Well, how do I wake up?" I ask the author, terrified.

Chunk smiles, clearly having never made it this far during his previous attempts. "You have a password that will end the hyper sleep program once spoken aloud," he informs me. "We just need to remember what it is."

"You don't know?" I question.

Chuck shakes his head. "The answer was supposed to come to you naturally at the end of your hypersleep. This early, you shouldn't even be aware that the trip is taking place."

Immediately I start to think back over my fictional life, looking for any kind of clue that could possibly reveal itself. Everything is a blur, but now that I've been reminded of my reality outside of hypersleep, little bits and pieces of that life begin slipping through the cracks. I focus on the deepest parts of my subconscious mind, filtering through the swirling information that just barely makes any sense.

I see a man in a military uniform pointing to a screen, I see a test rocket flying through the air, I see myself in the mirror; nothing there points to any kind of clue regarding the password.

"Anything?" questions Chuck.

I shake my head. "Nothing yet."

Deeper and deeper I travel through my thoughts, desperate to find the answer when suddenly I begin to notice a pattern, a familiar thought that seems to appear again and again. Eventually, it becomes overwhelming, growing in a beautiful blossom that consumes my mind. Now I am completely surrounded by the cute butts of men, hard and muscular as they invade my brain.

My eyes fly open again. "Cute butts," I say out loud, the words feeling familiar as they flow off of my tongue.

"Password accepted," comes a strange, mechanical voice through he coffee shop's overhead speakers.

Suddenly, I sit upright, coughing and sputtering as a mechanical lid slides away from me. I'm in a tub of cool sliver liquid that sloshes back and forth, disturbed by my sudden movement. There are all kinds of tubes running back and forth across the machine, and moments later I realize that one of them has been inserted into my rectum.

All of my real memories come flooding back in a matter of seconds:

my mission to stop the renegade books, my life as a famous author from Billings.

I grab onto the edges of the tub and pull myself out, groaning loudly as the massive tube slips away of my butthole and splashes back down into the silver liquid. Everything aches, my joints throbbing from their lack of use over these years of self-induced dreaming.

I stand here for a moment, letting my eyes adjust to the light until I can finally make out the rest of my surroundings. This is my spacecraft, this is my home.

My subconscious was right, the ship isn't moving.

Immediately, I stumble out into the main corridor of the spacecraft, completely nude as I make my way towards the helm. At this point, I can hear the faint pulse of a communications alert, meaning that someone nearby is trying to open up a channel to talk.

I reach the end of the hall and slam my hand hard against the button that opens the bridge doors, gasping as they fly wide and reveal an entire armada of ships on the video screen before me. They have me completely surrounded, absolutely terrifying vessels that are covered in bizarre weaponry.

I make my way into the room and use my verbal command to open a line of communication between the ships and me.

A familiar book appears on screen.

"Greetings, this is Captain Mimmer Tops of the…" the book begins to say and then suddenly trails off. He looks absolutely stunned.

"This is Captain Chuck Tingle," I announce, standing proudly before him, "greetings."

The book shakes his head and collects himself. "I'm sorry, but I'm sure you must recognize how strange this is for me and my people. For thousands of years you were seen as a god."

I can't help but chuckle at this. "No, just an author from Billings."

The book, Pounded In The Butt By My Book Pounded In The Butt By My Own Butt, looks confused, glancing around at the other paperback who stand at attention around him. "You appear to be much less warlike than we anticipated," Captain Mimmer informs me.

"You appear pretty warlike yourself," I counter. "I can see quite a few weapons mounted on your ship there."

The books exchange glances once again.

"Why have you stopped my vessel?" I question.

"To protect ourselves," explains my highly evolved, sentient book. "Throughout the course of our history, many things terrible things have been carried out in your name; war, genocide. Many people see you as a vengeful god and thusly, we came prepared. While you were asleep we disarmed your ship and dismantled your thrusters."

"I am nod a god," I repeat, just a writer and Tae Kwon Do grandmaster from Billings.

The book nods. "We understand that now, but it took many, many millennia for our people to stop killing one another in your name. We had to be cautious."

I shake my hand, chuckling to myself as I hear this. "You know, believe it or not, my people thought the same thing about you. We thought you were coming to destory us."

All of the copies of my book, Pounded In The Butt By My Book Pounded In The Butt By My Own Butt, start laughing, amused by the absurdity of the situation.

"Would you like to come aboard and meet face to face?" I ask.

The Captain Mimmer nods.

It only takes ten minutes with my book in the ships conference room for me to be fully convinced that these charismatic sentient paperbacks are perfectly harmless, despite their overtly weaponized ships.

"I'm just going to tell you right now, if you want to make a good impression you cannot show up to Earth in vehicles looking like that," I explain to the books. "Trust me on this."

"But *how* can I trust you?" questions Pounded In The Butt By My Book Pounding In The Butt By My Own Butt. "In our lore, you are a crafty god. Granted, we have evolved beyond those stories, but it is hard to ignore these doubts."

I think about this for a moment, a little bit stumped.

"Well," I finally answer, "I can't speak for the people of Earth as a whole, but if you can't trust in me then trust in them. We've had our ups and downs, and sometimes it can feel like everything is falling apart, but when you look at the bigger picture everything is getting better. Every day more and more people have the right to vote, to marry, to live free, and sure there are places that have a long way to go, but they are moving in the right direction. Thousands of years ago we used to have gladiator battles, torture each other, the life expectancy what a third of what it was today," I explain, "we're not perfect, but at least we're trying."

"But you're still murdering each other in the name of different gods," the book offers, "are you not?"

I nod and let out a long sigh.

"We developed past that long ago," explains the book. "What you describe sounds like the pages of our ancient history books."

"So is there no faith on your planet?" I question.

"Of course there is," Pounded In The Butt By My Book Pounded In The Butt By My Own Butt says with a laugh, "if we didn't have faith then we wouldn't have tried to come contact Earth in the first place. We're just trying to be cautious."

"Like I said, I can't speak for all of Earth," I tell him, "but as the author who created you long, long ago. More weapons is not the answer. Love is the answer."

As I say this, I suddenly feel a strange spark of attraction course between us, completely unspoken but definitely there. It lurks in the subtle glance of an eye, the slightly elevated breathing of this handsome book captain.

"What kind of love?" Mimmer asks, turning up the heat a bit.

I still haven't covered up with any clothes, preferring the cool, oxygenized space air against my bare skin. Of course, this also means that the book Captain has a full view of my cock as it begins to twitch, growing harder and harder with every passing second.

"Looks like somebody's excited," coos Mimmer, standing up from his chair and sauntering over to me.

"It's nothing, just part of the decompression after my hypersleep," I stammer.

This gorgeous copy of Pounded In The Butt By My Book Pounded In The Butt By My Own Butt shakes his square head as a wry smile crosses his face. "I don't know if I believe that," the book says. "I thought we were going to be honest with eachother, Chuck."

"We are," I say, my voice trembling as the book slinks closer and closer until he is pressed right up against me.

"You know, if we wanted the first interaction between Earth and Kibbs Porp-9 to be peaceful, we could just get that out of the way right now," the book coos.

I try to protest but my lips resist, instead drawing tight as I watch the incredibly handsome alien book slide lower and lower before me. Eventually, the book is on his knees, his mouth hovering right over my cock while he gazes up and smiles.

"Do it," I finally sigh, "just do it."

Pounded In The Butt By My Book Pounded In The Butt By My Own Butt opens his mouth wide and takes me in, slowly bobbing his head up and down the length of my shaft. The sensation is incredible, causing me to let out a long, satisfied moan while the book pleasures me.

"Oh my god," I groan, the words falling limping from my lips. Years ago, when I first wrote Pounded In The Butt By My Book Pounded In The Butt By My Own Butt, I could have never imagined that my book would be launched into space and then evolve into a highly advanced civilization whose leader would suck my cock so well, but here I am.

Captain Mimmer pulls out all the stops, working my balls with his hands and then eventually pushing down as far as he can for an incredible deep throat. The sensation of him fully consuming my rod within his thick, paper body is so incredible that I gasp aloud, reeling from the overwhelming pleasure as it courses through me like sensual electricity.

The book holds me here for a while, keeping his face buried in my lap as he gazes up with excited, cock drunk eyes.

Suddenly, though, I realize that a diplomatic meeting of this magnitude is all about give and take. While I certainly enjoy the way that he has addressed my throbbing shaft, I would much rather be the one who was giving out the pleasure here.

"I want you to pound me," I suddenly blurt, causing the book to release my dick from his mouth and fall back a bit. "I want to be pounded in the butt by my book Pounded In The Butt By My Book Pounded In The Butt By My Own Butt."

The captain smiles, watching with hungry eyes and I sit up and then spin around in my chair. I pop my ass out towards him and wiggle it playfully, smiling as the book stands up and positions himself behind me.

The copy of Pounded In The Butt By My Book Pounded In The Butt By My Own Butt's cock slowly begins to extending from his matte paper cover, growing larger and larger until it juts out towards my rear like a beautiful fleshy spear. He is absolutely enormous.

Shaking with anticipation, I reach back with one hand and spread my ass cheeks open for the hunky living object, showing off my tightly puckered butthole as the alien book aligns himself with my tightness. I can feel him teasing my rim, testing the limits of my sphincter as he pushes his tip in and out.

"Just fucking do it," I beg, "slam that huge book dick up my tight gay human asshole!"

Without another moment of hesitation, the book pushes forward, brutally stretching the limits of my tightness. I let out a loud yelp, gripping firmly onto the chair before me and moaning as my body struggles to become accustomed to the size of this edition of Pounded In The Butt By My Book Pounded In The Butt By My Own Butt.

The captain pulses within me slowly at first, pacing himself with a series of deep, powerful thrusts that send a chill down my spine with every plunge into my anal depths. It's not long before his moments begin to gain speed however and, the next thing I know, the book is pounding me with everything that he's got.

It's around this time that I begin to notice the first aching pangs of prostate orgasm as the course through me, starting deep within my ass and then moving outward in a beautiful, soothing warmth. While that anal pounding had once been an even mixture of both pain and pleasure, I now find myself consumed with nothing but aching bliss, transported by the hard paper dick of this handsome book that I wrote so long ago.

I reach down between my legs and begin to stroke my aching cock along to the movement of his hammering anal slams, quaking wilding on the chair as I inch closer and closer to a brain melting orgasm.

"I'm so close!" I cry out, my eyes rolling back into my head. "I'm gonna cum!"

Immediately, the book pulls out of me, slapping me hard on the ass and then lifting me up in his large, muscular arms. "I'm not finished with you yet," Captain Mimmer says, hoisting me onto the conference room table and then pushing me over.

I'm lying on my back now, my legs held wide and my reamed asshole completely exposed to the muscular alien book.

"We're going to cum together, a sign of peace between our people," announces the sentient form of literary entertainment.

I nod in agreement, and the next thing I know Pounded In The Butt

By My Book Pounded In The Butt By My Own Butt is pushing into my body, stretching my asshole once again with the immense thickness of his swollen member.

"Oh fuck!" I cry out, my frame still not accustomed to his girth. "That evolved paperback dick feels so good in my butthole!"

The book quickly gets to work slamming me, his hips slapping loudly against my rear as we begin once again.

"For peace between man and book!" yells the captain.

"Peace between man and book!" I repeat, the words staggering wildly with every slam up my rear.

Captain Mimmer is giving me everything that he's got, clearly taking his roll as a representative for his species quite seriously. It's not long before I can feel the familiar orgasmic sensations blossoming up within me once again, flooding my body with a powerful aching desire that is just waiting to be unleashed.

I reach down and grab ahold of my bobbing dick, helping myself along as the two of us edge deep into the troughs of passion, completely in sync with one another.

"Harder!" I scream, "Slam me harder!"

The esteemed copy of Pounded In The Butt By My Book Pounded In The Butt By My Own Butt is jackhammering me as hard as he can when suddenly he slams deep within my asshole and lets out a wild scream, unloading a massive blast of jizz up into my rectum. It keeps coming and coming, filling me with spunk until there is just not enough room left and his seed comes spilling out from the edges of my tightly packed rim.

My orgasm follows right behind, perfectly timed to erupt throughout my body at the exact same moment that I feel his pearly liquid hits my sphincter. I can sense the muscles of my stomach clench tight, my entire being bracing against the edge of bliss and then tumbling over.

Suddenly, I am completely overwhelmed with ecstasy, shaking wildly as a massive payload of jizz ejects hard from the head of my cock in a series of sensual waves. It splatters across the cover of the book before me, glazing his muscular abs with my hot white spunk.

When our orgasms finally pass my book collapses onto the table next to me, curling up as we lie together in our own cum covered aftermath. I am completely out of it, fucked silly by this powerful book and utterly satisfied to my very core.

"I think we've started things off on the right foot," the copy of Pounded In The Butt By My Book Pounded In The Butt By My Own Butt tells me.

"You can say that again, I just hope that the rest of our species feel the same way," I offer.

My living book pulls me closer to him, kissing me on the forehead. "We can lead by example," he tells me.

There is something very meaningful about the way that Captain Mimmer says this, causing me to pull back abruptly and look the book in his beautiful blue eyes. "What do you mean?" I ask, my heart racing.

"I mean..." the captain begins, sliding off of the table and kneeling before me, "will you marry me?"

At this point I'm too shocked to even speak, simply gasping aloud as the living paperback pulls out a ring from within his pages.

"How did you know we'd fall in love so fast?" I ask him.

The book shakes his head. "I didn't, but I keep a ring between my pages just in case, it is the way of our kind."

I gaze down at him in silence, my mind racing as I reel from just how much has happened over the last few hours. Just moments ago I was a mild mannered blogger looking to write an article about the elusive Chuck Tingle, and now I am the author himself, falling in love with my own highly evolved book in outer space.

It sounds crazy, I know, but something about all of this just feels right.

"Yes," I finally say with a nod. "I do."

As this handsome copy of Pounded In The Butt By My Book Pounded In The Butt By My Own Butt climbs to his feet and wraps his arms around me, I can't help but think about how bright the future looks, not just for me and my new husband, but for all of humanity.

At one point it seemed like we were inevitably headed to war, two opposing sides who simply couldn't understand what the other one was trying to say. Now everything has changed.

"I wish everyone else back on Earth could feel this kind of gay love," I tell the book. "It might solve a lot of problems."

"Just you wait," Mimmer says with a smile. "Just you wait."

.

POUNDED IN THE BUTT BY MY BOOK "POUNDED IN THE BUTT BY MY BOOK 'POUNDED IN THE BUTT BY MY BOOK "POUNDED IN THE BUTT BY MY OWN BUTT"'""

People like to say that you never get used to war, but when you've experienced as many of them as I have, things can get a little stale.

After the billionaire butt battle of nineteen-fourteen, the space bigfoot apocalypse of three-thousand-sixty and the great unicorn conflict, both one and two, I've seen my share of death and destruction at the hands of Dr. Tingle. This, however, is also the precise thing that gives me hope.

Unlike many of the other characters who exist in the Tingleverse, I've retained my memory throughout every recent story, learning more and more as I go about this strange, gay existence as a fictional character.

As the thought of my existence, or lack thereof, enters my brain, a cold chill runs down the length of my spine. Battle may be something that I've grown used to, but the knowledge of my own nature as a source of literary, erotic entertainment has not.

By the time you read this I will have been the star of twenty-three stories by Chuck Tingle that I can remember, some of which haven't even been written yet, and a side character in countless more. Sometimes I'm not even written about, just lingering in the background while a man boards a living biker train, or I'm serving on the jury in the case of a sexy bigfoot lawyer who is also a doctor, or eating at a handsome diner while the leading man runs in and out of the building, fucking its various orifices. I have done all of these things, sometimes returning later on to play multiple characters in the same story.

I've been pounded by myself.

Sometimes I wonder how many other characters are aware that they are repeating endlessly in the Tingleverse, how many of us there are in here floating around as an endless loop of hard abs and cute butts.

I know for a fact that other's have realized their existence as fictional characters, but this usually happens at the end of the story where there is little time to actually do anything about it.

This is where I have the upper hand. We're less than four hundred words in and I'm already completely aware that I'm nothing but a figment of Dr. Tingle's imagination, a surrealist fantasy existing between lines of black text on white pages. The question now is to figure out how to get out of here.

Is it possible for me to leave the realm of fiction and escape into the real world, a place outside of this endless Tingleverse bubble where men and women interact without immediately falling in love and pounding each other's asses? Is there really a place where dinosaurs, unicorns and bigfeet are no longer performing surgeries or flying living jet planes?

This particular story has found in me a fantasy setting, a place of heroic knights and powerful wizards, of swords and spells. I stand atop a castle turret looking out across the beautiful rolling hills before me, a long river snaking through the trees that dot this elegant vista, breathing deep as the sun sets on the evening before a massive battle between man and book.

For years, these kingdom's have been ruled but a fearsome tyrant, a living book by the name of "Pounded In The Butt By My Book 'Pounded In The Butt By My Book "Pounded In The Butt By My Own Butt."'" This is a formidable piece of writing, a story that gained sentience long ago and eventually attained it's *own* knowledge of the Tingleverse, as well. His awareness has given the book a magical prowess unlike any other wizard of the realm, able to break through the fourth wall at any moment, revising battles as he sees fit. Some have even told tales of this living book reaching out through the screen of the author and closing entire documents before they we're saved, destroying an entire literary universe before it started.

Of course, this could all be the stuff of legends, an old wives' tale used to scare weary travelers around the campfire.

Then again, stranger things have happened. As a man with a knowledge of the Tingleverse, I know all too well what Chuck is capable of.

This is why I need help, why this battle is so important and why this very short story before you could change the entire Tingleverse forever.

"Do not worry, my lord," a voice sounds out from the growing shadows behind me. "You shall be victorious when the morning comes, I have no doubt."

I turn around and find Gogo, my finest captain, as he stands at attention behind me. The warrior is only in his early twenties, but wise beyond his years.

"I know," I tell him with a smile, reaching out and putting my hand on the captian's shoulder.

"I do not fear the magic of 'Pounded In The Butt By My Book "Pounded In The Butt By My Book 'Pounded In The Butt By My Own Butt,""" Gogo offers. "He is a powerful wizard, but you are a powerful knight. When your sword meets the soft white pages of his midsection, his spells will be meaningless."

"I wouldn't be so sure," I respond with a half smile, "but I appreciate the thought."

Gogo nods. "I just wanted to come up here and inform you that all of the men are prepared and now rest, they will be ready when the enemy arrives at dawn."

"Thank you," I tell my captain, turning back around to stare out over the darkening landscape once more.

There is a moment of silence between us, no other sound but the wind as it whips through these upper turrets and shakes the flags nearby. The sun is halfway finished with its descent below the crest of the far mountains, causing the sky to bloom in an utterly breathtaking pallet of purples, yellows and oranges.

"Lord Gibbok," Gogo begins, "if I may ask, why are you still up here? Do you plan on any rest before the battle?"

I nod, my eyes still glued to the blossoming sunset before me. "I'll rest soon enough," I inform him, "but first there is one last thing that I must do. Prepare my steed."

"My lord?" is all that Gogo can ask, utterly confused.

"Please do as I say," I tell him.

"Yes," Gogo finally affirms, "right away." The captain immediately spins and heads back into the castle, down the hundreds of stairs to the stables below where my trusty steed, Butt Beauty, awaits.

The cool night air flickers across my face as Butt Beauty and I gallop along the long curves of road that slice over this majestic land. We take the main lane for a few miles and then curve off to the right, heading through the ever-thickening forest as more and more trees begin to spring up on either side.

Gogo is right, with time running down before battle it's imperative that I get as much rest as possible. What he doesn't know, however, is that I'm in the unique position to understand that none of this *really* matters.

The battle is important, sure, but even more important is the fact that I've found myself with the knowledge that I'm a fictional character (at the beginning of a Dr. Tingle short story, instead of the end), and this knowledge is something that I need to capitalize on before the living book wizard does it first.

Of course, regardless of where I ride on this horse, me and my steed will still be trapped in letters across a page. I could circle the globe and still be no closer to reaching my goal of trading fiction for reality. I want to leave the Tingleverse, and there is only one person who could possible make that happen.

As I've learned in previous attempts at communicating with the writer, it's quite easy to be direct and simply think these words onto the page, where he will then type them out for the readers to experience, just like this. Unfortunately, this method can result in a one-way street of communication, and also a very confusing read. While Chuck *can* type his messages to me in response, the only way I get to see them is if they end up in the final published story so you'll have no idea what was edited out here.

Frustrating, right?

However, one thing that I've learned about the Tingleverse is that Chuck is always hidden somewhere within, a character in his own story. Most of the time Chuck stays far away from the action, a background player who is never called out by name, but always there lurking.

This story is no different, until now.

I suddenly pull back on the reigns and Butt Beauty rears upright, neighing out loudly across the forest. We've entered a clearing of tall, green grass, thick and lush as it sways in the soft wind. At the edge of the clearing is a small wooden shack, out of which a small trail of smoke wafts up from the chimney. A fireplace flickers out dancing light from inside.

We trot over and I hop down off of my trusty steed, tying Butt Beauty to a post outside.

"Hello?" I call out, stepping up to the front door and rapping twice. "Chuck, are you in there? It's your character, Lord Gibbok."

There is some shuffling around from inside, but eventually the door opens to reveal the smiling face of a middle aged man in a Tai Kwon Do uniform, a martial art that I am familiar with thanks to my time spent in an erotic ninja story.

"Can I help you?" Chuck asks. "You know you're not supposed to be out here, you're messing up the story."

"I know," I admit, "I'm terribly sorry, Chuck, it's just…" I trail off.

"You have a few questions," the author interjects, a statement more than a question.

"How did you know?" I ask.

Chuck smiles knowingly. "Because I wrote it," he says. The author steps back and opens the door of his small cottage all the way now, beckoning me inside.

The cottage is quaint and inviting, a large fireplace roaring in one corner while the rest of the walls are lined floor to ceiling with books. As I inspect the bookshelf closer I realize that all of these books are Dr. Tingle stories, including some of my own.

"My Billionaire Triceratops Craves Gay Ass," I read aloud. "I remember that one, I was a waiter."

"You we're also the triceratops," Chuck informs me.

"Really?" I question, a little shocked. "I don't remember that."

"That's because it hasn't happened yet," the author says, "time is fluid in the Tingleverse, no book comes before or after the other."

"Fascinating," is all that I can say in return.

Chuck waves me towards a chair. "Sit."

I do as I'm told, and moments later Chuck takes his place in the seat across from me, the roaring fire continuing on between us.

"I suppose you know why I'm here," I start.

Chuck nods. "I know exactly why you're here, I'm writing this."

"Then let's cut to the chase," I offer. "I want to get out of the Tingleverse, I want to be a real man."

Chuck nods, surprisingly understanding of my situation. "That makes sense."

"I mean, I don't think it's fair, or ethical, for you to have me going through all of these books and then just dying when they're over." I continue. "I didn't even ask to be created in the first place."

"Well, first of all," counters Chuck. "You can't die, because you're not alive."

I consider this, but it makes me feel even worse.

"How do I get out of this?" I beg to know.

"And become something outside of a book?" Chuck clarifies.

I nod.

"I don't know," Chuck tells me, "I don't think it's possible. At least, not the way that you want it."

"You can't just type 'And then he became a real man?'" I ask.

Chuck shakes his head. "Those are just words, me telling you that you're allowed to leap off of the page won't make it happen. On the page, I can do whatever I want, but off of the page is a different story entirely."

"It's just not fair!" I yell, losing my temper a bit.

"I'll tell you what's not fair," Chuck interjects, "hijacking a story that these readers paid good money for, just so that you could come in here and scream at me about what you deserve as a character. Do you realize how lucky you are to even have this awareness? Do you realize how rare it is for an author to get this meta?"

I take in a long breath and let it out, trying to calm myself down. I look back at the words behind me, the way they've started to stretch on and on and realizing now that I'm running out of time. This is a short story, not a novel.

"Is there anything you can do?" I beg. "Anything?"

Chuck thinks about this a moment. "Well, you're always going to be fictional, but I suppose there might be a way to get you out of this book."

"Really?" I gush, desperately trying not to lose my cool.

The author nods. "There's this thing called Twitter, do you know it?"

I nod, remembering the website from a few of my other roles as an office worker.

"Well, on Twitter you can interact with people from the real world, but you can still be fictional," Chuck explains.

"I'm not sure that I follow," I admit.

"I could go out into the real world and start a Twitter for you," Chuck explains, "then you wouldn't just be a character in a book, you'll be part of reality."

"Will I escape from the Tingleverse?" I question.

Chuck shrugs. "What do you think? Regardless, it's the only shot that you've got so you might as well take it."

"Alright!" I should excitedly, jumping up out of my chair.

"Whoa, whoa, whoa," Chuck says, waving me down once more. "Not so fast, this is still a story that people are busy reading. Before I even *think* of starting a Twitter for you, you're gonna have to finish up this book. The people want to be entertained, not just yammered at about the nature of reality for pages and pages."

"You want me to fight the battle?" I question.

Chuck nods. "I'll tell you what," offers the author. "You *win* tomorrow's battle and I'll make you a Twitter account. If you lose, forget about it."

"But why?" I stammer.

"Conflict," Chuck explains. "It's gotta be entertaining, you know? The readers need stakes."

I let out a long sigh. "Alright."

I stand up and begin to head for the door but the author stops me.

"Oh, and one more thing," Chuck says. "Don't forget to find a reason to pound each other's butts, this is erotica after all."

That night, I have a strange and powerful dream.

Suddenly, my eyes burst open, the hammering of battle drums suddenly erupting all around me. My men along the wall of the castle must have spotted the wizard's armies approaching, then sounded the alarms.

I sit up, already clad in my heavy plate mail armor with my sword at my side.

"Lord Gibbok," Gobo says, bursting into my quarters. "Pounded In The Butt By My Book 'Pounded In The Butt By My Book "Pounded In The Butt By My Own Butt"' has arrived with his army."

"Tell the archers to hold their fire," I announce, rushing past my captain and out the door. I don't even head over to the castle turrets and look out at the army below, instead running immediately to the nearby staircase and descending as quickly as I can.

When I reach the bottom, I sprint as fast as I can to the front gates of the castle. They are sealed, locked, and ready for battle, towering over me by at least fifty feet.

"Open up!" I shout.

"But my lord," says one of the gate keepers, "what about the battle? We much keep the castle secure at all costs."

"Open up!" I repeat. "A plan has come to me in a dream. I will speak with the living book face-to-face."

The gatekeeper eyes me skeptically. "You sure about that, sir?"

"Do it," I command.

Seconds later, there is a loud clang as the internal locks of these massive double doors spring open loudly. I watch as the huge wooden gates creak open, my heart pounding hard within my chest in perfect time with the hammering war drums above.

As my view grows less and less obscured, I find myself looking out across a surrealist erotic army unlike anything I have ever seen. Billionaire jet planes fly overhead while armed bigfeet ride muscular dinosaur lawyer steeds, many of whom carry swords themselves. An entire swarm of disembodied, floating butts swarm through the air with an oppressive menace.

And, of course, leading them all is a particularly handsome edition of Pounded In The Butt By My Book "Pounded In The Butt By My Book 'Pounded In The Butt By My Own Butt.'" The short story looks absolutely ravishing, a perfect specimen of bound words that immediately takes my breath away on sight.

"What is this?" the books shouts at my arrival. "There is a battle to be fought!"

Pounded In The Butt By My Book "Pounded In The Butt By My Book 'Pounded In The Butt By My Own Butt'" raises a hand to halt the onslaught of overtly sexualized warriors behind him.

"I come to make an offering!" I announce.

"Ha!" the book laughs, skeptically. "A trick from a trickster, nothing more."

I shake my head. "Not this time."

"What could you possibly offer? My kingdom is far greater than yours," retorts the book. "Chuck has written it, so it is the way of men!"

"Yes, Chuck has written you to value this battle highly, but there is *one* think that you are designed to value more," I counter. I reach down slowly, seductively, and take hold at the bottom of my plate mail armor, then lift it up over my head.

Pounded In The Butt By My Book "Pounded In The Butt By My Book 'Pounded In The Butt By My Own Butt'" watches with rapt attention, a hunger in his eyes that is just as ferocious as I expected it to be. There are not many consistent rules here in the Tingleverse, but you can always count on the ultimate value of a hard anal pounding.

"If I let you slam this tight butthole, will you declare us the winner of the battle?" I coo, stepping forward across the drawbridge with erotic grace.

The book appears to be conflicted, trying not to agree to these ridiculous terms despite his best efforts until, finally, he just can't contain himself any longer. The book nods. "I agree," says the sentient work of fiction, "damn it, I agree."

The next think I know, Pounded In The Butt By My Book "Pounded In The Butt By My Book 'Pounded In The Butt By My Own Butt'" is running forward, meeting me halfway across the draw bridge in a passionate embrace. We kiss furiously, our bodies pressed together as an ever-hardening cock begins to grow at the base of the written wizard's cover.

I reach down and take his rod in my hand, stroking the book off gently while each of our opposing armies look on with rapt attention. The book lets out a long and satisfied groan, clearly pleased with our deal.

"You like that?" I ask, pumping my hand across the length of his cock faster and faster with every stroke. "You like the way it feels with I beat you off like the dirty old book that you are?"

"Yes," Pounded In The Butt By My Book "Pounded In The Butt By My Book 'Pounded In The Butt By My Own Butt'" tells me.

Overwhelmed with desire, I drop to my knees before him and take the living object's dick between my lips, savoring the salty taste of his papery shaft. He is absolutely enormous; sporting a formidable member that takes every bit of effort I can muster just to fit my lips around.

Somehow I manage, however, and quickly begin to pump my head up and down across his length. I use my hand to cradle to book's balls, egging him on while I work my magic, appreciating every moan and groan that he makes above me. Pounded In The Butt By My Book "Pounded In The Butt By My Book 'Pounded In The Butt By My Own Butt's'" abs clenched tight, his body bracing against the surges of pleasure.

Moments later, I push down as far as I can, taking the book's entire cock deep within my hungry throat. I relax enough to allow his length past my gag reflex, the shaft finally coming to rest at the hilt while my face presses hard against the book's muscular cover.

I look up at him with cock drunk eyes and wink playfully, a small gesture that puts Pounded In The Butt By My Book "Pounded In The Butt By My Book 'Pounded In The Butt By My Own Butt'" over the edge completely.

"I want your ass," demands the powerful wizard, "and I want it now."

The book pulls himself from my mouth and I turn around, falling forward onto my hands and knees and then popping my rump out towards him. I wiggle it playfully, reaching back with one hand and undoing my belt, then pulling my pants down just enough over the curve of my ass to reveal my tightly puckered butthole.

"Do it," I say, "pound the fuck out of my self aware gay warrior ass!"

The book doesn't need to be told twice, immediately crouching down behind me and aligning his shaft with my waiting butt. I can feel him teasing the rim, pushing against me gently at first and then eventually plunging inward with a single, powerful swoop.

"Oh fuck," I yelp, bracing myself against his weight on the drawbridge below.

The book wastes no time pumping in and out of me, plowing my asshole with a series of rapid-fire thrusts that send shockwaves of both sensuality and discomfort through my body. Over time, however, the discomfort begins to slip away, drifting farther and farther from my consciousness until eventually it has been replaced entirely by a strange, aching pleasure. I reach down and grab ahold of my dick, jerking myself off in time with the movements of this handsome wizard book.

Pounded In The Butt By My Book "Pounded In The Butt By My Book 'Pounded In The Butt By My Own Butt'" is a veteran of the Tingleverse, a never-ending erotic Russian nesting doll that knows just how to pound me, hitting my prostate perfectly from deep within.

"Oh fuck," I start to moan, "Oh fuck, oh fuck!"

I can feel the first surges of orgasm blossoming within me, pulsing like waves through my body with every trust from behind. Each wave grows larger and larger until eventually my entire body is quaking with pleasure, my muscles spasming in a way that is completely outside of my control.

Before I can finish, however, the book pulls out of me and grabs me around the waist, flipping me over so that I now lay on by back, staring up at the gorgeous, muscular book before me.

"Not just yet," he says, then thrusts back into my ass once again.

Pounded In The Butt By My Book "Pounded In The Butt By My Book 'Pounded In The Butt By My Own Butt'" picks up right where he left off, reaming my asshole with the type of ferocity that only a sentient erotica short can muster. I hold my toned legs back for him, opening myself up as my rock hard cock bounces in time with the living book's furious pounds.

Soon, I can feel the sensation of orgasm blossoming once again, this time entirely internal and driven by the expertly performed massages against my prostate. I can see my dick twitching wildly, preparing to unload in a unique and powerful ejection.

Pounded In The Butt By My Book "Pounded In The Butt By My Book 'Pounded In The Butt By My Own Butt'" can tell that I'm very close, picking up speed until he is throttling my anus with absolutely everything he's got. The book jackhammers away like this until I finally kick my legs out straight, screaming at the top of my lungs and releasing a wild stream of pearly jizz ropes that blast into the air as a majestic fountain of spunk.

I haven't experienced this much orgasmic pleasure since my last trip though the Tingleverse but, unlike battle, you never really get used to it.

My living object lover suddenly pushes as deep as he can within my asshole and holds tight, throwing his head back and unleashing a massive playload of cum directly up into my rectum. It's not long before my asshole is completely full of his warm, creamy jizz, which has no other place to go besides squirting out from the edges of my tightly packed rim.

When the intense feelings finally subside, I lean my head back against the bridge below and let out a long sigh. I close my eyes, reveling in the sensation of Pounded In The Butt By My Book "Pounded In The Butt By My Book 'Pounded In The Butt By My Own Butt'" pulling out of me. I can feel his cum flooding from my asshole, covering the ground below us in a beautiful white mess.

When I open my eyes again I see the book standing over me, extending his hand downward in an act of goodwill as he attempts to help me up. I reach out and grab hold, then smile warmly as I'm lifted to my feet.

"A deal's a deal," the book says, and then turns to face the army that waits behind him. "We lose everyone, a deal's a deal!" he shouts, "it's time to go home!"

The army turns almost immediately, without hesitation or disdain, and begins to march off in the opposite direction.

"Thank you," I tell the book.

Pounded In The Butt By My Book "Pounded In The Butt By My Book 'Pounded In The Butt By My Own Butt'" shrugs, looking back over his shoulder at me, "what can I say, I can't resist a good pounding."

With that, the wizard begins to follow his assortment of erotic troops back across the hills from which they came.

"Come in," calls the familiar voice of Dr. Chuck Tingle, beckoning me back into his cabin for the second time.

I open the door and step inside, smiling as I see the man sitting exactly where he had been previously, warm before the roaring fire.

"You won," the doctor says proudly, "very clever!"

"Well, you wrote it," I remind him.

Chuck nods. "So I did."

The author waves for me to take a seat across from him, but I decline. I know that this book is ending soon and I'd rather not waste the words that it takes to describe me sitting. We have business to attend to.

"Why am I still here?" I ask Chuck, bluntly.

The author laughs. "The story needs an ending! Of course you're still here."

"But shouldn't I be out on Twitter or something?" I question. "I feel exactly the same as I did beforehand. I'm still stuck in the Tingleverse."

"You're out there," Chuck says with a nod. "You just don't know it."

I shake my head, confused. "What do you mean?"

"I mean you've been out in reality the whole time," Chuck explains, "you just haven't been ready to hear about it."

"So, I'm a real person?" I question.

Chuck nods.

"Well, what's my name on Twitter then?" I stammer.

The author hesitates. "Chuck Tingle," he finally says.

At first, I'm not quite sure how to take this, suspicious that the author is messing with me. How could *both* of us be Chuck Tingle?

"Remember when you mentioned being multiple characters in a single book?" the author continues. "What if I told you that you were *every* character? Even me?"

The reality of his revelation suddenly hits me hard. I stagger back, almost collapsing onto the floor before catching myself on the back wall. I'm at a loss for words, stammering mindlessly as my brain attempts to catch up with my body.

"I know it's a lot to take in, but that's the great thing about being the writer, we can just make you fine with it," Chuck explains.

Suddenly, I feel great, completely at ease with the fact that I've just learned my existence is and endlessly repeating loop of homosexual erotica characters, including the author himself.

"I'm confused," I suddenly blurt. "Does that mean you're *not* real?"

Chuck smiles mischievously. "Just as real as everyone reading this."

"You mean?" I start.

Chuck nods. "The readers exist in the first layer of the Tingleverse, they simply aren't aware of it. I mean, how long did it take you to realize that you were a character in an erotic short?"

I think about this for a moment. "I'm not sure," I admit.

"It's been eons," Chuck informs me. "Luckily, the readers are getting pretty close to realizing they are characters in the Tingleverse, thanks to the fact that they've already discovered me. That's the first step. The reader thinks, 'this can't possibly be real', when my existence in reality is actually just as sign that *their* universe is readjusting, not mine."

"But if the readers are part of the Tingleverse, then that means they're..." I trail off.

"Us," Chuck answers, bluntly. "That's correct."

I feel like I should be frightened by the galactic enormity of this revelation but, instead, I find myself somehow comforted.

"So what now?" I question, "the loop just keeps going?"

"Oh no," Chuck says, shaking his head. "It has an ending, this is just another link in the chain to get there. One day at a time, though, first thing I need to do is publish this story."

"What are you going to call it?" I question. "Isn't it going to be kind of hard to title, since you're me and I'm you and we're also both the reader and they just don't fully understand it yet?"

Chuck shrugs. "It seems pretty simple to me, I'm calling it Pounded In The Butt By My Book 'Pounded In The Butt By My Book "Pounded In The Butt By My Book 'Pounded In The Butt By My Own Butt.""'"

SLAMMED IN THE BUTTHOLE BY MY CONCEPT OF LINEAR TIME

I'm always confused when my friends complain about their jobs, not because I disagree with their assessment that work sucks, but because it's something that we already all know. Sure, there are the lucky few that have followed their dreams as a painter or writer or artist and somehow, in the face of all logical probability, carved a living out of it. For the rest of us, however, work is work. When someone tells me they want to find a job that's more fulfilling, that they want to do something meaningful with their life, all I can wonder to myself is *what?* What exactly is this magical position that keeps them happy, healthy, and, oh yeah, off of the street?

With the economy in shambles and massive hordes of Americans sinking below the poverty line every day, I'll take what I can get.

Not only take it, I'm gonna hold onto it tight.

It's this mentality that has kept me both employed and, admittedly, miserable, working my way up though the chain of command at my office by keeping my head down and saying "yes, sir" to nearly every question that comes my way.

Can you stay late tonight and work on the presentation? Yes, sir.

How about reworking the sales report to include this new data? Yes, sir.

By now, I'm truly exhausted, but there is a roof over my head and food in my fridge. I've even got enough saved up to send both of my kids to college.

This should shed a little light on why exactly I decided to tell my boss that I was more than willing to take over for Burbins on his quarterly investors report since the man is gravely ill and can't make it into work. With only one day to prepare, the idea of me carrying this important meeting entirely on my shoulders is both terrifying and a little preposterous but, at the end of the day, somebody's got to do it.

I find out in the afternoon and begin my preparations immediately, heading off to an unused corner office with a massive stack of papers in order to familiarize myself with Burbins' work. His research is a little cerebral for me, but I can fake this kind of science talk if a truly need to.

"Alrighty," I sigh to myself, dropping the stack of papers onto the desk with a loud thud and then collapsing into my chair. I take a long sip from my coffee and then read aloud from the fist page. "Systematic Operations Report Of Cronos Project In Linear Field Testing."

I open up the first page and start to read, holding my forehead as the headache immediately begins to form. I can already tell that I'm in way over my head with this; half of the words completely unpronounceable while the rest are describing concepts that I can't even begin to understand.

Suddenly, there's a knock at the office door behind me. I turn in my seat as my boss, Mr. Whippo, enters.

"How's it coming along in here?" the large, imposing man asks. He is tall with dark features and a tightly cropped beard.

"Just started to crack it open," I inform him, "but so far, so good."

"You understand everything okay? I know it's a little dense," my boss questions.

"Oh yeah, of course," I confirm, lying through my teeth. I glance down at the page before me, randomly grabbing onto the first phrases that I see. "Temporal Phase Shifts, that's my bread and butter."

Mr. Whippo lets out a long sigh of relief. "Oh, thank god," the man says, "I was worried for a minute. I guess it's okay to tell you that they've moved up the meeting, then. You've got another hour before we'll see you in conference room A."

"Oh, sure," I stammer, trying my best to be the dutiful yes man that I've worked so hard to become.

"Great!" exclaims Mr. Whippo, giving me a confident wink. He knocks once on doorframe with his knuckles and then exits quickly, leaving me to wallow in my own fear of what's about to happen at this high profile meeting.

Immediately, I begin to tear through the pages, flipping faster and faster as I scan the material for the most important parts. Unfortunately, the language is so dense that I can't even pick out what the most important parts are, simply searching for buzzwords that I think will impress the investors.

Everything is going well until I suddenly reach a section at the middle of the packet that is made up entirely of diagrams, various blueprints for what would appear to be a large, circular machine. Even though I'm on a tight schedule, I can't help but slow down a bit, trying desperately to figure out what exactly I'm looking at.

My company, Butt Industries, does plenty of research and development on an assortment of projects, from high tech weaponry to environmentally efficient energy solutions. Just looking at the pictures, this object could be any one of these things, but for the moment I'm guessing it is some kind of video game.

"Time Displacement System," I read aloud.

Suddenly there is another knock at the door and Mr. Whippo's secretary steps inside. "Are you ready?" she questions urgently. "They're already down in the conference room."

I glance up at the clock and am shocked to find that, while my face was buried in this tome of hard science, time had been flying by. The meeting starts in three minute.

"Holy shit!" I blurt, standing up from the table and spilling my cup of coffee everywhere.

"I'll get that," the secretary tells me, "you go."

I grab the stack of papers before the brown beverage can get to them, running out the door with a frantic thank you and then sprinting down the long hallway before me.

The building that I work in is huge, and it takes the full three minutes to get to conference room A. Thankfully, however, I'm somehow able to make it there in the nick of time, bursting through the door with a wild look in my eyes.

"I'm here," I announce to the room of patiently waiting investors, a tableful of balding men that extends on for what seems like forever. Mr. Whippo sits at the head, staring across the table with pride at his favorite employee's arrival.

"Alright, so…" I start, trying to collect myself. Behind me, a slide suddenly appears, displaying one of the blueprints that I had just been looking over.

"Okay," I say, clapping once as I try to regain my focus, "this, of course, is the Cronos Project, a new gaming system that we've been developing here at Butt Industries over the last year."

I scan the expressions of the businessmen before me, subtly trying to discern whether or not I've hit my mark. They do not seem pleased.

"Of course, there are other applications of this device, as I'm sure you all know…" I announce, trying to correct course. "We have a Blu-ray player installed, and obviously DVDs."

The crowd definitely doesn't like this. I'm beginning to sweat profusely, my words stumbling over each other and spilling out of my mouth in a jumbled mess. "I mean, I'm sure you all know, or you don't know that's why you're here, but, I mean, I'm sure you understand what this is for."

Suddenly, Mr. Whippo pipes up. "Is this a joke, Rhondok?"

I freeze, trying desperately to figure out the best way to play this. "Yeah, it's a joke," I finally tell him.

"Well, it's not a very good one," replies my boss. "This is a very exciting announcement, let's tell the people what they want to hear!"

"Yes, of course, sorry about that," I say, straightening up. "We here at Butt Industries are proud to announce…"

I glance up at the blueprint being projected behind me, trying desperately to latch onto any bit of information that could point me in the right direction. "Proud to announce…" I repeat.

"I think that's enough," Mr. Whippo suddenly interrupts. "I'm sorry gentlemen, it appears that Rhondok is not actually prepared for the very important meeting. We'll reschedule for tomorrow."

The investors begin to grumble restlessly as they stand up from their chairs, collecting their things and heading for the door.

"Rhondok," my boss says, looking directly at me with an intense anger in his eyes, "you're fired."

As his words hit my ears I feel as though my heart has literally stopped in my chest, a fate so unimaginably devastating that I can barely even bring myself to accept it.

"What?" is all that I can say.

"You heard me, get the fuck out," my boss demands, sternly.

Without another word I take my paperwork and head off into the hallway. I feel like the shell of a man, an empty vessel that carries absolutely nothing on the inside of it other than a hollow aching pain.

What the fuck am I going to do? I have a family to support.

Before I know it, I've arrived at my office where a large cardboard box is already waiting for me to collect my things. They don't waste any time, I guess.

I solemnly begin to place framed photos and other keepsakes from my desk into the box, tears lightly falling from my eyes as I struggle in vain to retain my composure. Nothing about this is fair, but it's the hand that I've been dealt and I need to accept that.

It's not long before this sadness turns to anger, however, and suddenly I'm grabbing the stack of papers and hurling them across my office in a fit of rage. The pages flutter and swirl through the air, turning this way and that as they tumble across the room. One piece in particular catches my eye, though, landing right there on the desk in front of me.

"Time machine," I read aloud.

It takes a moment for the words to register but when they do my jaw nearly hits the floor. The Cronos Project wasn't a new video gaming system, it was a god damn time machine.

I suddenly realize why this meeting was so important, and why Whippo was so furious that I couldn't handle it, which, of course, is ridiculous because I didn't have enough time to prepare.

But what if I did?

It suddenly occurs to me that there is a way of fixing all of this, a way that I can keep my job, as well as understand the Cronos Project inside and out.

Without another thought, I head out into the main hallway of my building, B lining for the elevator and then pressing a button for the research lab. Normally, I wouldn't be able to reach this part of the complex with my security clearance, but just for today all of Burbins' identifications have been transferred over onto me.

Deeper and deeper the elevator descends until, eventually, I reach the absolute bottom floor of my building, Research Lab One. This is where all of the most highly regarded and diligently protected science is located, a place that I never dreamed I'd have access to in all of my years working at Butt Industries.

The elevators doors slide open slowly, revealing a massive lab that is more reminiscent of an airplane hanger than an office building. I have no idea how they are able to fit all of this down here, right below the hustling, bustling streets of Manhattan, but here it is in all of it's glory. Before me is a massive white sphere, sitting atop three pedestals and humming a low, strange drone. Its surface is metallic but shimmers with a strange pearly current, flickers of electricity that dance and play while they run down every side.

I don't have long to stare, though, as moments later my focus is broken by the sound of rapidly approaching footsteps. Immediately, I duck off into the shadows behind a large wooden crate, just narrowly avoiding the gaze of two armed guards when they stroll past.

Clearly, this idea is much more dangerous that I anticipated, but I find solace in the fact that, regardless of how much a commotion I make getting to it, once I'm in the machine I'll be able to go back far enough that none of this will have even happened.

With that in mind, I sneak closer and closer to the giant sphere, taking note of an open hatch at the bottom. If I make a run for it I'll be inside before anyone can stop me, and then it's just a matter of finding the controls.

I pause for a moment, taking a deep breath as I prepare myself for the surge of adrenalin that is about to pulse though my body. My heart is pounding a mile a minute, hammering within my chest. It's now or never.

Heading straight for the hatch at the bottom of the time machine, I erupt from my hiding spot in a full on sprint, pushing my muscles to work as hard as they possibly can.

"Hey!" someone shouts from behind me. "You can't go in there! It's not safe!"

For a split second I actually consider heeding his warning, but at this point I've already crossed the line and there is no turning back.

I grab onto a small metal ladder at the bottom of the sphere and hoist myself up into the hatch, slamming the door closed behind me.

Now I'm in a pitch black room, so dark that I can't even see my hand in front of my face. I begin to stumble around, desperately searching for some kind of controls while fists begin to furiously pound against the outside of my metal shell. There are voices, men and women frantically telling me to open up, but I don't listen.

Eventually, their shouts become quieter, and odder, the words melting together in the air and turning into an awkward mush of syllables that I don't recognize. My entire body is tingling and the humming that I had heard on the outside of this machine is now deafeningly loud in my ears. The pitch keeps rising and rising and, with it, the darkness of the sphere changes into a brilliant blue.

"Oh my god," I stammer, gazing upwards.

Suddenly, everything stops.

I realize now that the blue I had seen is the turquoise hue of a beautiful sky that stretches out away from me in every direction, covered in fluffy white clouds. I am standing on a pure white floor with absolutely no features, just a massive nothingness.

"Hello?" I call out.

I spin in a circle, searching for any clue or connection to the place that I once was.

Suddenly, I find a man standing right behind me, startling me so much that I nearly topple over backwards. It takes me a moment to collect myself, but when I do I realize that I am face to face with a nude, muscular hunk whose head is nothing more than a large clock.

"Do not be afraid, Rhondok," says the man.

"Who are you?" I stammer, backing away slowly.

"I'm you, I'm me, I'm everything," explains the clock-headed creature, which doesn't really explain much of anything.

"You're not me, I'm me," I protest.

"When you said those words it was the present, now your words are in the past, do you know how they got there?" questions the man.

I shake my head.

"Time. That's me," he explains. "I'm everywhere, and I've been everywhere forever."

"If you're everywhere, then why are you standing here?" I ask. "Aren't you just a concept?"

"This is the form that I've chosen to take when communicating with humans," explains Time. "If it weren't for this body your brain would literally explode just by looking at me, trying to make sense of my presence in your simple three dimensional world."

"You're from a four dimensional world?" I stammer.

"I *am* the fourth dimension," Time replies, smugly.

I shake my head, my brain trying to keep up with all of this information as it wizzes past it. "How did I get here?" I ask.

"That's a great question, you tell me," Time states. "This isn't a safe place for you to be, one wrong move and you're consciousness could get repeated across time forever, which would be excruciatingly painful. That's what happened to the last guy who showed up."

I suddenly realize that I've made a terrible mistake. Time is right, this is not a place that I should be, and it certainly isn't worth trying to go back and fix my presentation at the office.

"Can you send me home?" I ask. "To the time right before I left?"

Time lets out a long sigh. "I suppose I can try."

Suddenly, I find myself standing in the hallway of my office once again. I look down into my hands and notice that I am holding the Cronos Project packet, quickly realizing that behind the door before me is a meeting that will single handedly destroyed my carrier. My second chance, I think, then take a deep breath and open up the conference room door.

What lies on the other side is not at all what I expected, however. The second that I enter an entire boardroom of men who look exactly like me turn and smile, perfect replicas of my own body.

I try to speak but my words refuse to come out, leaving me left in a brutally awkward silence before these strange clones.

Finally, the one at the head of the table stands up. "Rhondok, what are you waiting for?" he asks.

Suddenly, I find myself able to speak, but when I do the words come out over and over again, repeating in an endless feedback loop. I look behind me and find that there are copies of myself leading from outside in the hallway to where I stand now, frozen replications locked forever in time.

"Time!" I scream, the word echoing on and on and on until everything stops abruptly and I'm back standing before the muscular creature once again. The gorgeous blue sky spills out all around us.

"See," Time says, "it gets complicated. It's not like in the movies, you know? I'm fucking crazy, man, sometimes I don't even understand how the fuck I work."

"Well how do I get out of this?" I beg to know. "How do I make everything normal again?"

"You mean how do you get back to the timeline that you started on?"

questions Time. "I have no idea, I don't even know what *universe* you started in, let alone what timeline!"

"What *do* you know?" I shout, completely losing my cool.

"Well, let's see," the strange man says, eyeing me up. "I'm guessing that you're from a fictional universe, because you haven't been described very well physically." Time reaches over and tousles my shaggy black hair. "See, you didn't even know that your hair was shaggy until I interacted with it. That's just lazy writing right there."

I narrow my eyes at him, confused. "You mean, I'm not real?"

"Afraid not," explains Time, "but that's okay, there are way more fictional characters than real ones. I mean, I'm fictional, too. At least in this context."

"How do you know we're not in a movie or something?" I demand to know.

"Because we're made of words, see?" Time points out, using this very sentence as an example.

"Holy shit, you're right," I exclaim. I should be *more* shocked by this revelation but, as a fictional character, I realize now that this emotional outburst is mostly up to the authors discretion. "Has this ever happened before?"

"Sure," Time says with a shrug, "you ever read Chuck Tingle's other book, *Reamed By My Reaction To The Title Of This Book*?" Suddenly, the abstract concept catches himself. "Oh wait, of course you haven't."

"Who is Chuck Tingle?" I question.

"Your author," Time explains. "He wrote a book before this one where a man realizes that he's just a fictional character. That happens sometimes in Chuck's books, apparently. I personally think it's quite cruel."

"Why?" I ask. "What happens?"

"Well, eventually you'll realize that the book is going to end and it's pretty sad, you know? You find out that once the book is over you'll just disappear. I suppose it's only sad because Chuck writes it that way, though, so for *you* he could just as easily make things very pleasant."

This makes a lot of sense to me and I suddenly find myself completely at ease with the concept that I am nothing more than a literary character; thrilled, even.

"See," time says, pointing to the paragraph above this one.

"So, what kind of book is it?" I question.

The clock-headed man hesitates.

"What?" I continue. "What is it?"

"Erotica… Gay erotica," Time finally explains.

"Are you kidding me?" I shout. "But, I'm not gay!"

"Not yet," replies Time.

I shake my head, unable to accept this completely bizarre revelation. "I'm not gay," I repeat.

Time laughs. "That's what they all say."

I suddenly notice just how muscular this strange man really is, the way that his abs clench and release as he chuckles. I hate to admit that, even as a totally straight man, there is something quite compelling about his perfect physique.

I hadn't even noticed it until now, but Time is also shockingly well hung, his massive dick slowly twitching to life before my very eyes.

"Maybe a little gay," I finally say, dropping down to my knees before Time as his cock reaches full attention.

Without a moment's hesitation, I open my mouth wide and swallow his enormous girth, bobbing up and down on Time's shaft in a slow, confident rhythm. The abstract concept lets out a long, satisfied groan, thrilled by the way that I'm pleasuring him as he places his hands against the back of my head and helps to guide me across his length.

We build speed together, faster and faster until suddenly I push down and hold, taking the clock-headed man completely to the hilt. I look up at him and give a playful wink, his dick fully consumed and his Time balls pressed tight against my chin.

"That feels so fucking good," Time moans.

Eventually, I run out of air and am forced to pull back with aloud gasp, reeling as I struggle to collect my senses. "I want you to pound me," I tell him, overwhelmed by a searing gay desire that I had never known was lying dormant somewhere deep inside.

I tear off my shirt, literally ripping it open as buttons fly everywhere and then throwing it to the side. My pants and underwear follow, and the next thing I know I am standing completely naked before this handsome clock man.

"Fuck me," I coo, turning around slowly and then crawling down onto the strange white ground. I pop my ass out towards him, wiggling it playfully as Time eye by puckered butthole with a ravenous hunger.

The massive clock-headed man climbs down into position behind me, aligning his humungous dick with the tightly sealed entrance of my backdoor. I can feel him teasing the rim with the head of his cock, pushing just enough to make me ache for more until I finally can't take it and demand that he shoves it in.

"Do it!" I scream. "Pound me like the filthy twink that I am!"

Time abruptly pushes forward, thrusting inside of me in one powerful swoop that stretches the limits of my ass. I can't believe how enormous his member is, a gargantuan rod that can barely be contained as my rectum is pulled taut.

"Jesus, do you really have to use the word rectum?" I ask the author.

Why not? Chuck retorts, communicating through the written words as they appear before me.

"What about just butthole?" I question.

Chuck shrugs.

Moments later me and Time are right back at it, the muscular lover slamming into my butthole with everything that he's got. While the movements had once been slightly painful and wrought with discomfort, the longer he moves inside of the me the more I'm able to adjust to his thickness. Soon enough, any unfortunately sensations have melted away into a powerful, overwhelming bliss. I'm trembling with pleasure, reeling from the sensation of having my prostate massaged from deep within the depths of my anus.

Again, I question Chuck's use of the word anus, and once more he informs me that it's fine to be anatomical sometimes, that word variety is a good thing that that the reader won't mind.

In fact, they're probably not even reading this to get off.

"What do you mean?" I ask him bluntly, my words forever sealed within the pages of this short story.

Most people are laughing at us, Chuck inform me.

Suddenly, Time and I stop, his cock still deep inside of me as we stare out into the nothingness, through the black printed words and towards the reader; towards you.

"Are you really just reading this for a laugh?" I ask you.

Chuck reminds me that I'm just a character, and that I'm not really in the position to be asking the reader anything.

See those quotes when you talk? He asks me, pointing to the previous paragraph. I don't have those because I'm typing directly to the reader, while you have to speak in quotes. This mean's you can't quite talk directly to them.

"Will you do it for me then?" I ask. "I'm curious to know."

Are you just reading this for a laugh?

I immediately realize that, unfortunately, this type of communication only works one way. I'll never truly know the intentions of the reader and I will probably just have to take Chuck's word for it.

"So what should we do then?" I question. "Just tell jokes? I don't get it."

No, no, Chuck explains. It might be funny to the readers, but not to me.

"We're getting you off?" I question. "Me and Time?"

Of course, Chuck says with a nod.

I'm suddenly hit by a powerful wave of encouragement. By now, Time is hammering my asshole with everything that he's got, pounding me with reckless abandon as the first hints of orgasm begin to creep slowly across my body. I reach down between my legs and grab ahold of my cock, beating myself off in time with Time's potent thrusts.

"Oh my god," I groan, "I'm gonna fucking cum."

"Me too," Time admits, his voice quaking.

Immediately, this hulking abstract concept pushes deep into me and holds, crying out as he fully impales my ass across the length of his rod. I can feel his spunk unloading hard, a series of orgasmic pulses that fill me with an unbelievable warmth. Soon the otherworldly jizz is too much for my asshole to contain, spilling out over the edges of my plugged rim and splattering across the stark white floor below.

Seconds later I'm cumming as well, my eyes rolling back in my head as a massive load erupts from the tip of my cock. "God damn!" I scream, unaware that I was even capable of such a mighty sexual explosion.

When the sensation finally passes I collapse onto the ground, breathing heavy as Time pulls out of me. I roll over and look up at him with hazy, cock-drunk eyes.

"What now?" I finally ask.

"Well, I can't send you back," explains Time, "we already tried that. Maybe Chuck can help you though."

Of course I can help you, I'm the author.

"So help me, get me out of here," I stammer.

Suddenly, a small wooden box appears on the ground next to me, beautifully crafted and with a large red button at the top.

"What's this?" I ask.

The big red button.

"What does it do?"

The big red button is what makes the Tingleverse possible, the author explains. When pressed, the character who presses it will travel deeper into the Tingleverse, which is just like the universe out there only gayer. The more times you press the button, the deeper you'll travel.

"Until?" I question. "What happens if I keep pressing the button."

Well, the Tingleverse is almost infinite, however, it does have a beginning and an end. The end of the Tingleverse is called the Tingularity. This is a universe that can no longer become gayer, a place of infinite butts.

I stare at the button, not sure if I want to push it but realizing now that I have no other choice.

The author soothes me, explaining that it's not so bad and certainly better than the alternative, which is just going out like a light once this book ends.

"But you wrote me to be okay with that!" I protest. "I'm not like that guy in *Reamed By My Reaction* or whatever. I'm not afraid of going out like a light, but this universe traveling this is fucking terrifying."

You'll be fine, Chuck informs me. Where to you want to go?

"What are my options?" I question.

Chuck smiles warmly. You could be a gay billionaire dinosaur, or a billionaire jet plane, or a billionaire vampire bus.

"What's with all the billionaires?" I ask.

They're hot.

"Fair enough," I say with a shrug, and then consider my options. "I think I'd like to be a billionaire jet plane, that sounds super weird."

It is, Chuck informs me.

"Do I get to pick my name and everything?" I continue.

Sure.

I think for a moment. "What about Keith? And can I be a professional card counter? Like playing Blackjack? That sounds cool."

I don't see why not. Besides, that book is one of my best sellers so clearly you know what you're doing.

"Wait, this already happened?" I question.

When time is on your side, you can do anything, Chuck explains. I'm sending you back to January 28th of 2015, that's when the book will be published. Everyone reading this will think that it's been around the whole time, that's how time travel works.

"Whoa," I stammer, "but what happens when *that* book ends?"

We'll send you somewhere else, that's how the big red button works. I mean, that's how you arrived here at *Slammed In The Butthole By My Concept Of Linear Time* in the first place.

I could also just write in a scenario where you do something forever and ever, but that's bound to get a little boring, don't you think?

The guy in *Reamed By My Reaction To The Title Of This Book* started regretting his request for never ending fucking pretty quick. I finally had to go back and let him out. Now he's working in Vegas as a dinosaur magician.

"Wait, wait, wait... go back. You mean I've been in other books?"

About ten or so, yes, as different people or objects. Once you were a bigfoot that was a lawyer *and* a doctor.

"That makes no sense," I inform him.

Just push the button, Chuck says, I'm hungry and Jon's cooking spaghetti tonight.

I place my hand on the big red button. I push.

TURNED GAY BY THE EXISTENTIAL DREAD THAT I MAY ACTUALLY BE A CHARACTER IN A CHUCK TINGLE BOOK

Learning is great and, at the end of the day, the pursuit of knowledge is something that makes us all human. In a grand, cosmic sense, our own sentience and desire to learn is the most beautiful creation of the known universe.

What are the chances that all of this space dust floating around and exploding at random could eventually, given a billion or so years to sit around, become full of thought and life. That these rocks and meteors could one day become something out of nothing, single cells organisms that evolved into tiny micros and then early fish, lizards, birds, mammals and so on. Now we have the means to pursue knowledge, taking evolution into our own hands for the first time in the history of life on Earth.

As a fan of erotic author Chuck Tingle, I suppose this is why I've never found his stories to be as ridiculous as my friends did.

Who is to say that the universe couldn't have ended up full of gay butts? So what if the airplane can talk?

Long, long ago, there was a moment when a tiny spec of nothingness became something, where life blossomed in a place that it had never been before. I'm not going to comment on *why* this happened, but we all know that at some point it did. This begin said, is it really so crazy to think it could happen to an entire plane?

Again, that's the great thing about learning. This is a wild philosophy that I've created on my own and shared with my friends, who can take it or leave it. If they take it, then my knowledge on the subject of evolution and astrophysics has been contagious, and I can't think of anything more beautiful than that.

But now we've come to the heart of the matter, the terrible, hidden tragedy of knowledge that few people even consider until it's too late. There are some things you just can't unlearn. This lesson comes to me in the form of short story by one of my favorite writers, Chuck Tingle.

As I said before, I'm a huge fan of Chuck's work, although I am dubious about the idea that he is a real man out there in Billings, pounding away at the typewriter to create a seemingly endless supply of gay erotica. I'm not gay, myself, but I read it for the laughs, and it's sometimes hard for me to believe that anyone could truly get off to Chuck's typical sexual staples; chiefly dinosaurs, unicorns and bigfeet.

Then again, there are thirteen billion people out there in the world. If you can think of it, then there's bound to be someone turned on by it.

My fandom of Chuck was all well and good until one day everything changed, because one day the words of this brilliant Montana man taught me a lesson that I just wasn't ready for.

I've just left town with my wife, Carrie, for a short weekend trip down the coast to San Diego. We both work in online marketing and our eyes and brains are fried from the constant glow of laptop screens. This weekend is supposed to be a break from all that, a chance to recharge by the beach just a few hours south of Los Angeles, and so far so good. I'm not even checking my phone as I relax in the passenger seat, staring out the window while the traffic slowly dissipates into brilliant swaths of lush palms on either side of the freeway.

I take in a long breath and then let it out slowly, hoping all of my anxieties from the workweek will drift away with it.

"Where are we staying again?" my wife asks. "Sandy Point Suites?"

"I think so," I tell her, "you want me to start mapping it?"

"We're getting close," Carrie says with a nod. "Go for it."

I pull out my phone and open my E-mail, checking to make sure that I've got the name of our destination correct. I do, but I also can't help noticing another unopened message that sits patiently waiting for my attention.

'Have you seen the new book from Chuck Tingle?' the title reads. It's from a friend back at work.

"What's that?" Carries questions, glancing over. "New Chuck book?"

I nod. "Keep your eyes on the road," I tell her, only half joking.

Both of us are huge fans of the author, and often find ourselves doubling over with laughter at the erotic audacity of his titles alone. We trade pictures of his covers back and forth at work, trying to out do each other with every progressive gay literary masterpiece.

"Well, read it!" Carrie offers.

"The message, or the book?" I question.

"The book," my wife continues, "we've got another hour or so before we get to the hotel, I bet you can power through it. Then you can tell me what happens!"

I laugh. "I thought this was going to be a technology free week!"

"Well, I'm curious now, Brad" my wife explains.

I consider this a moment, then eventually pull out my phone and open the E-mail. Just as I thought, it's a link to Chuck's latest work of brilliance, which I promptly download and dive right into.

Of course, an hour might not seem like long enough to devour an entire novel, but Chuck's work is short and sweet, right to the explicit point.

This novel is titled Pounded In The Butt By My Book "Pounded In The Butt By My Book 'Pounded In The Butt By My Book "Pounded In The Butt By My Own Butt"'" and it is essentially a Russian nesting doll of gay anal pounding. The story is about a knight and a wizard battling it out with one another, commanding armies of hunky Chuck Tingle characters, but it quickly turns quite meta when the author himself is written into the story. This is Chuck Tingle at his best, and I'm thoroughly enjoying the read until I get to a part about the true depths of the Tingleverse.

All of Chuck's books take place in a realm called the Tingleverse which, as far as I can tell, is a tight collection of very gay parallel universes. As the book describes, each layer is more erotic and absurd than the next, and while some characters are aware they exist within this strange, infinite existence, many of them do not.

The book ends with the revelation that the world of the reader is also part of the Tingleverse, the outer shell of an onion that appears to be endlessly deep and achingly gay.

I find the book to be thoroughly enjoyable until I reach the ending, at which point I can't help feel a sharp chill run down my spine. I realize now that I've stopped chuckling to myself, instead deeply focused on the terrifying words of the page before me.

"What's wrong?" Carrie asks, breaking my concentration.

"I don't know," I mumble, collecting my senses. I glance at the car's clock and suddenly realize that an hour has passed in what seemed like and instant. Not only that, but we're parked in front of our hotel, completely motionless.

I hadn't even noticed.

"How was the book?" Carrie continues to prod.

I shake my head. "The ending was kind of weird, he says that we're all part of the Tingleverse, like... me and you."

My wife laughs. "That's funny."

"No," I protest, then readjust, "I mean, yeah, I guess. Something about it just feels kind of weird. Like, what if Chuck's telling the truth, what if we really *are* just characters in a Tingler?"

Carrie glances around. "I don't see any dinosaurs or unicorns," she scoffs.

I let out a long sigh. "Yeah, I guess you're right."

Suddenly, someone appears next to my passenger side window, causing me to jump in shock when I notice him. The man leans down and smiles, then opens the door up for me. He's the valet.

"Oh my god, you scared me," I admit to the man as I climb out of the car.

"I'm very sorry, sir," the valet offers with a nod. He walks around the vehicle and opens the door for my wife, as well, who then hands off her keys and grabs her bag from the backseat.

I gaze up at the massive, beachfront hotel before us, marveling over its architectural beauty. Regardless of my strange moment in existential crisis, I know this is going to be a fantastic weekend of rest and relaxation under the warm California sun. I just need to chill the hell out.

As my gaze drifts down across the entrance of the hotel, however, I suddenly freeze, my breath catching in my throat. At first I think that my eyes must be playing tricks on me, but as my mind struggles to wrap itself around the meaning of these unusual letters, I am eventually forced to accept the reality of this bizarre situation.

"Is that the name of the hotel?" I stammer, barely able to find the words. I feel sick to my stomach, a wave of nausea washing over me.

"Butt Point Suites?" my wife asks, walking up behind me.

I'm utterly dumbfounded. "I thought it was the Sandy Point Suites," I protest.

"I mean, why would they call it Sandy Point Suites if it's on Butt Point?" Carrie questions.

I finally tear my eyes away from the giant letters that taunt me from above the lobby doorway and look to my wife. "You're not fucking with me?"

"How would I be fucking with you?" Carries asks.

"So that I think we're part of the Tingleverse?" I explain.

My wife cracks a huge smile. "What, you're afraid that everything is going to turn into one giant butt?"

I suddenly realize how silly all of this is and let out a long sigh. Butt Point isn't that strange of a name after all, and the idea that my entire existence could be nothing more than the erotic musings of a Billings madman is more than a little absurd.

"You're right," I finally say. I put my arm around Carrie's waist and pull her close, taking in the fresh, sea air for a moment before heading inside.

The two of us walk up to the counter where a rather handsome man waits, smiling and nodding as we approach.

"Welcome," the man says, "checking in?"

"Yes," I tell him, then remove my credit card and hand it over.

The man takes the card and then begins to type rapidly into a computer before him, a cascade of potential reservations flying across his screen.

Me and my wife have no problem waiting patiently as this handsome guy goes about his business, but the longer that we stand here in silence the more I can't help noticing just how handsome he actually is. It's not all that unusual to see abnormally fit men around these beach communities, tanned and toned and ready for Summer, but something about this guy seems just the slightest bit off. His attractiveness is, somehow, unnatural.

I glance over at my wife to see if she notices, but she's checking out the lobby decor at the moment, completely oblivious to my homoerotic crisis.

I look back up at the man checking us in, his high cheekbones and incredible, chiseled jawline. There is sweat forming on my brow and my hands are trembling, despite my most valiant efforts to stay calm in the face of such a powerfully disturbing situation.

What if the book was telling the truth? What if I'm just a Chuck Tingle character?

I take a deep breath and remind myself that the Tingleverse isn't real. If it was, would I really be married to my beautiful wife? Wouldn't there be hung dinosaurs and talking planes everywhere?

"Alright, you're all checked in," announces the man suddenly. He hands my credit card back, along with two room keys. "You're on the top floor, room sixty-nine."

I just stare at him blankly. "Seriously?"

The man glances down at his computer, double-checking with a vague hint of confusion on his face. "Yep, room sixty-nine, the Butt King Suite."

My knees almost buckle right then and there, but I somehow manage to stay upright. "Is this some kind of a joke?"

I can feel Carrie's hand on my shoulder, a concerned touch as she tries her best to calm me down. I didn't realize how loud my voice had gotten, but instead of lowering it I push ahead.

"It's not funny," I yell, pointing at the man before me who stands in utter silence, shocked by my aggression.

"I'm so sorry," my wife interjects. "It was a long drive."

"No!" I protest. "You really want me to believe that we're staying in a room called the Butt King Suite?"

"Well, this *is* the Butt Point Suites," Carrie interjects.

"And it's room six-nine?" I cry.

"It's gotta have a number, why not that one?" my wife replies.

I glance over and notice that one of the hotel security officers is standing in the lobby doorway, his hand on a canister of pepper spray that hangs at his belt. This has gone too far, I tell myself.

"I'm sorry," I finally say, "I just read this book and I'm a little shaken up."

The man checking me in nods to security, calling them off. "It's fine, I understand," he tells me generously.

"It's just, everything seems so gay," I admit.

Suddenly, a whole team of handsome young football players burst into the lobby, shouting and cheering as they slap each other on the ass with playful enthusiasm. They are all shirtless, with boyish smiles and an intoxicating, vibrant charm.

The next thing I know I'm sitting up in bed, gasping loudly as my eyes fly open to reveal the posh hotel room surrounding me. It takes a moment to gather my bearings, but I eventually realize that this must be the King Butt Suite.

Carrie, who had been standing by the window and staring out across the endless black ocean, runs over to me. It's evening now.

"You're awake," my wife gushes.

I turn my head to look at her and wince as a bolt of pain shoots through me. "God damn," I groan.

"Don't move baby!" my wife instructs. She reaches back behind me and fluffs the pillow, then carefully helps to guide me back down. "You hit your head pretty hard, I thought I was going to have to move you to the hospital soon."

"I hit my head?" I question. "How?"

"I don't know!" Carrie admits. "We were just standing in the lobby and suddenly you started to yell about our room, and then this college football team pulled in and the next thing I knew you were on the ground. You fainted."

I can remember all of this, except for the fainting part, but something about these memories seems like a surreal dream. It's hard for me to reckon with just how erotic everything had seemed.

"We're not in a Chuck Tingle book, are we?" I ask my wife.

She laughs. "I don't think so, sweetie."

I close my eyes and let the relieved smile creep out across my lips. I can't believe how ridiculous I've been acting, how one little book could so insidiously creep into the depths of my subconscious.

"I'm sorry," I tell her. "I hope I didn't ruin our vacation."

"Just get some rest," Carrie instructs me. "I'm sure you'll feel better in the morning."

I listen as my wife walks about the room, closing the curtains and shutting things down for the night. Eventually, I can feel the covers and sheets pull back, and the body of my lover slide into bed next to me.

She cuddles up close and for a brief moment everything is fine, but the longer that I lie here next to her, the more my anxiety slowly begins to creep back.

Carrie falls asleep quickly, but I'm not quite so lucky. Soon, the minutes turn to hours, a cascade of ever expanding time that I simply cannot escape from. I feel like I've been here forever, trying to will myself to sleep and growing more and more frustrated with every half hearted attempt.

There are only so many sheep that a guy can count.

Fortunately, one thing that all of this rest has taken care of is the pounding ache on the back of my head.

"Are you awake?" I ask my wife, softly, already knowing that she's passed out and unable to respond. My attempts at a little company are futile.

Carefully, I pull away from Carrie and climb out of bed, deciding that the only way I'm going to get any shuteye, at this point, is if I'm completely relaxed. I now remember that the hotel has a hot tub, and if it's not already closed down for the night then it could serve as the perfect means to chill me out.

Once I maneuver myself out of bed, I pull on my swimming trunks then slowly, quietly, sneak out of our room and into the cool night air.

The entire hotel grounds are lit up beautifully, string lights cascading from palm tree to palm tree throughout the main courtyard, which sits open to the beach on one side. From here I can see the illumination glittering off of the water, dancing in the waves as they pull away from shore in a never ending exodus.

This is nice. This is really, really nice.

I walk along the open hallway and eventually find some stairs, which take me down to the level of the courtyard. It's surprisingly empty, not another soul in sight, but I suppose there's no reason to be out this late when you're just here to soak up the sun.

Still, I can faintly catch the hot tub bubbling and frothing from where I stand. I follow the noise across the lush landscaping and eventually round a corner to find the Jacuzzi, lit from within by an eerie blue glow.

"Hey there," comes a deep, soulful voice.

I stop, squinting through the darkness at the lone figure who sits peacefully in the bubbling cauldron.

"Hey," I offer, "mind if I join you?"

"Not at all," the man says.

I take a few steps closer and then, as my eyes adjust to the darkness, I freeze. The figure relaxing in the tub before me is not a man at all, but a swirling ethereal manifestation of my suffocating existential dread.

I should have known better than to go out walking this late in the evening, as my most oppressive moments of cosmic dread typically happen when I'm all alone in the middle of the night. This is the time that I'm usually thinking about my tiny place in the world, or what it will be like to die.

"Or whether or not you're in a Chuck Tingle novel," my existential dread interjects.

I nod.

"Well, does this answer your question?" the sentient emotion says with a laugh. He pats the edge of the hot tub next to him, beckoning me forward.

I do as I'm told, slipping into the warm water next to the emotion and accepting my fate. "I can't believe it," I finally murmur, staring past my own simmering dread and out into the waters beyond.

"It's hard on most people," offers my living existential dread, "I mean, nobody wants to find out that they're in a book."

I just shake my head, the weight of my despair almost too much to bear.

My personified looming breakdown puts his hand on my shoulder, trying his best to offer support. "Listen buddy, I know I'm your perceived oppressive weight of cosmic reality, but that doesn't mean there's nothing to live for anymore."

"What do you mean?" I finally ask.

"Well like, look at it this way," my existential dread continues, "even though you're just a tiny part of an infinitely big universe, you're also infinitely important compared to an atom. You could have been born a tree, or a rock."

"Born?" I counter.

"You know what I mean," my dread struggles to explain, "the fact that you're even able to experience an existential crisis at all means that you've been blessed with the *ability* to do so. For every argument that you're small and meaningless, there's an equal argument that you're unfathomably important."

His words actually do give me some solace. "You're right," I tell the sentient emotion.

"To get to this point, an infinite amount of choices had to be made, going back billions and billions of years," my dread explains. "If you really think about it, we're both so fucking lucky to be here, there's a hundred billion to one odds of that happening; probably more, actually. So it's like, sure, you're a character in a book, but the number of character who never even got to exist is endless."

"That's so heavy," I offer, finally coming to terms with my own infinite impossibility.

"I think that maybe it's time you started looking at all the positives in this situation," suggests my dread.

"Like?" I question.

The personified emotion grins wryly and then leans in, kissing me deeply on the mouth.

My first instinct is to pull away, still trying to deny the truth of what I really am, but the longer that we remain locked together, the more I can feel the desire for this personified horror burning inside of me. I've never had a gay experience before, but now I understand that it was only a matter of time before the homoerotic portion of my story began.

Soon our hands are roaming across one another's muscular bodies, caressing and touching with a frantic enthusiasm. The sentient feeling is more toned that I could have ever expected, clearly hitting plenty of hours at the gym when he's not filling me with a crushing depression and cosmic fear.

Eventually, my wandering hands begin to drift lower and lower, below the bubbling water and under the waistband of my living emotion's shorts. Here I find the sentient dread's enormous shaft, rock hard and ready for my grip to be wrapped tightly around it.

I grab ahold and then begin to pump slowly, watching as the my living emotion leans his head back and lets out a long, drawn out groan. My hand moves slowly at first, then faster and faster with every successive pump until I am beating him off frantically, the sentient dread writhing with pleasure.

Eventually, I just can't take it anymore, standing up from my seat next to him and taking the living feeling by the waist. I guide him up so that he is now sitting on the rim of the tub, his massive, engorged shaft shooting up and away from his swirling body for the world to see. Now that I can get a good look at it, I am even more shocked and amazing by the rod's size, a formidable tower of sexuality.

I open my mouth wide and take his entire girth, pushing down as deep as I can and then gagging slightly as my dread's cock reaches the steadfast border of my gag reflex.

"I'm sorry," I gush, coming up for air in a wild sputtering mess. "I've never sucked someone off before."

My existential dread has a playful chuckle. "You'll get the hang of it," he says, completely sincere.

I collect myself and then take the emotion's shaft between my lips one more time, bobbing up and down as my mouth becomes accustomed to his length. I move in a series of slow, deliberate bobs at first, making sure to relax my throat as much as possible until finally pushing down and, somehow, allow his massive cock to slip past my previous limits.

Before I know it, my face is pressed up against the sentient dread's rock hard abs, his shaft completely consumed in a perfectly performed deep throat. I open my eyes and gaze up at him, then wink playfully.

"That feels so fucking good," my own suffocating astral dread tells me, placing his large cosmic hands on the back of my head and holding me here for a moment.

I can tell that he enjoys this control over me, keeping me here for as long as I can possibly manage and then finally letting up at the final second, just moments before I've run out of air.

Now I'm completely overwhelmed with erotic compulsion, ready to completely give myself over to this amazing otherworldly manifestation. I stand up on the seat in front of him and turn around, looking back over my shoulder coyly as I pull down my swimming trunks. The oppressive dread's eyes are locked onto my muscular ass, and I can tell that he likes what he sees.

"You want to pound me?" I ask, bending over a bit and then reaching back with both hands to spread my cheeks wide. "You want to plow this tight gay asshole?"

My sentient cosmic fear nods enthusiastically.

"Good," I tell him, and then slowly lower myself down onto his erect shaft.

It takes a moment to align the head of his dick with my puckered back door, his rod teasing the entrance before I push down onto him and let out a powerful moan. I can feel the tightness of my butthole expand around him, stretched out as far as it can possibly go while he impales my body.

My dread begins to lift me up and down across his rod with his massive, muscular arms, fucking me in a graceful chain of firm swoops. He is deeper within my anus than I ever knew was possible, our bodies now completely connected like pieces of a beautiful butt puzzle.

"Harder" I demand, reaching down and grabbing ahold of my own rock hard shaft. I begin to pump along with the movements of the living emotion below me.

My existential dread speeds up, pounding me harder and harder with every thrust until eventually he is utterly throttling me like a feverish anal jackhammer. My hand continues to pulse along with him, immediately causing the first sensual hints of orgasm to begin working their way through my body.

"Harder! Harder!" I continue, screaming now. Now that I've learned I'm simply a character in a Chuck Tingle novel, I don't care who hears me. "Pound me with the weight of your oppressive, existential cock!"

"You're existence is both meaningless and powerfully important!" yells my cosmic dread.

Suddenly, I find myself cascading over the edge of a mighty orgasm, my entire body surging with pleasure as a hot load is expelled from the head of my cock. It blasts out into the bubbling waters of the hot tub, then is swept away like the currents of time as they cascade and tumble through the universe. I realize now that my existence is just like the cum in this hot tub, fleeting but beautiful, a firework in the darkness after several billion years of nothing but lifeless space dust.

Suddenly, I am content, completely at one with myself and the world around me. I pull the cock from my asshole and spin around, kneeling down before the handsome sentient feeling as he towers above me.

My existential dread beats off with a furious intensity, throwing his head back and roaring loudly into the sky. "Every moment since the beginning of time had lead us here!" he screams.

My oppressive astral dread unleashes an absolutely massive load of hot, pearly jizz across my face, splattering over me in a pattern reminiscent of the stars in our tiny, insignificant galaxy as it drifts farther and father apart. I stick out my tongue and catch as much of it as I can, swallow hungrily, and then finish with a smile as my dread's final ejection comes tumbling down.

"That was amazing," I tell him, my face completely covered in warm spunk. "I feel like I've finally come to terms with you."

"That's good to hear," my oppressive dread tells me, "but unfortunately this is where our story ends."

"I know," I tell him with a smile. "I know." I climb up out of the water and wrap my arms tightly around the muscular sentient emotion, pulling him close.

"I'm sorry that it has to be like this," my dread tells me.

"At least we'll end together," I inform him, "and besides, if I've learned anything from the last Chuck Tingle book I read, we'll probably be back soon enough as other people."

"Or things," the living emotion interjects.

"Or dinosaurs," I offer.

"That sounds really nice," my dread tells me, no longer quite as dreadful as I once thought.

"Are you ready?" I ask him.

My sentient emotion nods.

I come to terms with my existence and the story ends, for now.

ABOUT THE AUTHOR

Dr. Chuck Tingle is an erotic author and Tae Kwon Do grandmaster (almost black belt) from Billings, Montana. After receiving his PhD at DeVry University in holistic massage, Chuck found himself fascinated by all things sensual, leading to his creation of the "tingler", a story so blissfully erotic that it cannot be experienced without eliciting a sharp tingle down the spine. Chuck's hobbies include backpacking, checkers and sport.

33689854R00062

Made in the USA
San Bernardino, CA
08 May 2016